CAPTIVA CABANA

CAPTIVA ISLAND
BOOK TEN

ANNIE CABOT

CABOT PUBLISHING GROUP

ISBN ebook, 979-8-9894164-2-4

ISBN paperback, 979-8-9894164-3-1

CHAPTER 1

 *M*aggie Moretti looked at her husband Paolo's face and smiled. Leaning against the stone wall, she watched his expression and could tell he was content. Being back in the small Italian town of Gaeta, Italy, she could feel her husband's soul-deep connection to his homeland. The town was in his blood, and she understood that as much as he loved living on Captiva Island, Gaeta was closest to his heart.

She sighed and crossed her arms against her chest wondering if she'd have trouble getting him to return to Florida after Ciara's wedding.

"You love it here, don't you?" she asked.

Paolo nodded. "I have so many memories that fill my heart. How can I not?"

Maggie smiled. "I understand. Andover, Massachusetts, isn't Gaeta, Italy, but I too have moments when I miss the place I lived for most of my life. Maybe we should come back here more often. I think you need this."

Paolo turned away from the Mediterranean Sea and leaned up against his wife.

"What do you mean?"

She shrugged. "I have eyes, don't I? Ever since we arrived, you've been pensive...very alone with your thoughts."

He pulled her close. "Have I? I'm sorry, I didn't mean to shut you out. In fact, I love this town more when I'm sharing it with you. The truth is that I've been thinking not just about me, but my sister."

Maggie's brow furrowed. "What about? If you're worried that she's making a mistake..."

"No, nothing like that. I'm happy for her. I like Crawford very much."

"So do I. I think they make a wonderful couple. What's got you so concerned?"

Paolo shook his head. "Not concerned. I'm not sure how to explain." He hesitated before speaking. "Were you as surprised as I was that she wanted to come back home to have her wedding?"

Maggie laughed. "Well, it was a bit shocking considering how adamant she was to leave Italy in the first place. I know she loves Gaeta, but Captiva is her home."

He nodded. "Exactly. I didn't think Gaeta meant so much to her. Now that we're here and she's about to walk down the aisle, all I keep thinking about is that she's going to fall in love with this place all over again, and..."

Smiling, Maggie suddenly understood. She turned and hugged Paolo to comfort him. She tried not to laugh, but she couldn't hold back a small giggle.

"What's so funny?" he asked.

She pulled back and looked into his eyes.

"Your sister has no intention of moving here. Captiva Island is her home now. If you're worried that your sister is going to leave you and return to Gaeta, you can stop fretting. She wanted to get married and make memories here, nothing more. Is that what's been keeping you from sleeping?"

He smiled. "You noticed that, did you?"

"I felt you get out of bed last night and sit by the window. I thought you were just reminiscing about the past and your childhood. I had no idea you were worried that your sister was going to leave you."

He sighed. "The truth is when I say that out loud it sounds ridiculous. But, you know me so well, am I acting like a foolish old man?"

Maggie laughed and put her arm through his. "Not foolish."

They both laughed at her point.

"Do you really believe that Crawford would leave his business and family in Captiva and move permanently to Italy?" she asked.

"I didn't say what I was thinking was reasonable. It's just a knee-jerk reaction. Don't worry, I'll calm down."

Maggie kissed his cheek. "Maybe you should tell Ciara how you feel. It wouldn't hurt for the two of you to have a heart-to-heart. I honestly think you have nothing to worry about, but a nice quiet talk with your sister might make you feel better."

Paolo nodded. "I don't want her to think I'm crazy."

"Sweetheart, your sister knows you very well. There is no way she'll think anything but that you love her and want her in your life. Come on. Let's get inside. I believe the bride is ready for her brother to walk her down the aisle."

They started for the house but Paolo stopped and pulled her into his arms. He took her face in his hands and gave her a lingering kiss. He then pulled back and smiled.

"No one is luckier than I to have such a wonderful wife. I love you, Maggie Moretti."

Tears welled in Maggie's eyes. She'd been kissed by Paolo many times, but somehow, standing in front of the Mediterranean Sea made this one all the more romantic.

She'd been through much in her life, but Maggie now believed in miracles. Every step along her journey had brought her to this small Italian town, and into the arms of Paolo Moretti.

She rubbed his arms. "And I love you," she responded. "Now, let's get this party started."

. . .

Ciara Moretti steadied herself against her brother Paolo as she climbed the stone steps leading to the Church of Saint Francis of Assisi. Her matron of honor, Sarah Hutchins, handed her bouquet to Crawford's daughter Becca as she straightened the long lace veil behind her.

When they reached the entrance to the church, Ciara looked beyond to the Mediterranean Sea and remembered running up these very steps as a child.

As a young girl, she believed there was nothing beyond the gates of the city. She'd play up and down the streets, kicking balls and chasing her friends. Occasionally she'd run down to watch the fishing boats come into the port.

When she was a teenager, she and her friends would sit on the stone wall and watch the fishermen work on the dock. One such fisherman was Lorenzo Barone, a young boy who used to sit beside her in school. He had stopped attending classes when his father put him to work on their boat. He'd caught her eye more than once, but both of them being too shy, they did nothing but smile and nod when in each other's presence.

As smitten as she was with Lorenzo, Ciara was more curious about his travels than anything else. Every morning she'd watch Lorenzo and his father sail away from Gaeta's port as she imagined him arriving at exotic and faraway places.

Ciara would ask him questions about these destinations and when he had nothing more to tell her other than the number of fish they'd caught that day, she finally understood. Realizing that none of his adventures went much farther than where his father dropped anchor to fish, Ciara gave up asking questions and turned her attention to reading stories about far away destinations.

Even though her head was in the clouds, her parents kept her feet firmly planted in Gaeta. They expected her to remain at home until she found a husband. It was her responsibility to care for her parents. That was the role of every young Italian girl in the town.

Ciara wanted something more, and so, when she was in her early twenties, and desperate to leave Gaeta for America, Lorenzo asked her to marry him. Her heart torn, she wouldn't give him an answer right away. Her parents insisted that she accept his proposal, but instead, Ciara did what no one saw coming.

She was convinced that she'd never leave Italy if she married Lorenzo. She liked thinking about him as her friend and nothing more. If he had asked her only two years earlier, she might have considered it, but now, there was nothing to be done but quickly leave for America.

Her parents disowned her, which broke her heart, but the pull to the United States was strong and so she left her little town and went to America. She didn't look back at either Gaeta or Lorenzo, but instead looked forward to her new life in a new country.

She found work as a domestic on Captiva Island working for Rose Johnson Lane. When her brother followed her to America, she helped him start a new business on the island of Sanibel. Keeping busy by helping Paolo as well as working for Mrs. Lane left little time to think about romance or dating.

She'd gone on a few dates over the years, but nothing ever came of them. When she was forty years old, she stopped dreaming of finding the one love that would last forever. There was one man from her hometown who corresponded with her online. He even proposed to her, but his motive was to gain Gaeta property through inheritance. Ciara saw through his reasons for the proposal and sent him packing and back to Italy.

Ciara was convinced that marriage and motherhood would never be in her future. At least that's what she believed until she met and fell in love with Crawford Powell. Crawford had been married before and was a widower with four grown children. The owner of Powell Water Sports on Captiva Island, he was loved and respected among the islanders.

Since she, along with her brother, worked part-time for Rose Johnson Lane caring for her property, it wasn't unusual to pass Crawford's shop on the way. They'd wave to each other as she passed by, and Ciara considered him a friend. Over time their friendship developed into something more.

Everyone who saw them together could see that Crawford was in love. It took a while before Ciara could see it for herself, and though she didn't dare believe that he'd ever propose, she was content to be with such a kind and loving partner.

When Crawford got down on one knee in front of all their friends and family, Ciara was over the moon with happiness. This was what she'd begun to dream about, and Crawford made her dream a reality.

Now, standing in front of the church door, she took a deep breath and turned to her brother Paolo. "Are you ready?"

Paolo smiled. "I'm ready if you are."

Ciara turned to look at Sarah. "Here we go."

There was never any need for formal invitations as the church bells signaled that a celebration and mass was about to start. With the reception in the outdoors of the town square, tradition meant there would be more food and music than anything Ciara and Crawford could have prepared.

Smiling from ear to ear, Ciara tried to control her emotions. Normally not one for wearing lots of makeup, she let Sarah add false eyelashes and foundation on her already flawless skin. The last thing Ciara wanted was to cry her makeup off.

As she and Paolo walked toward the front of the church, she kept her eyes focused on her groom. With an occasional glance to the right and left, she stifled a laugh when she realized that half the town filled the pews. Her wedding was turning out to be the event of the year in Gaeta.

Maggie and Chelsea looked like they were going to cry as she passed. Ciara stopped to hug Maggie. The wedding would never have happened without her support. In fact, the entire island of Captiva had a hand in bringing Ciara and Crawford together.

Ciara returned to Paolo and when they reached the altar, he leaned toward her and kissed her face before placing her hand in Crawford's. Paolo walked to the front pew and sat next to Maggie.

Ciara felt her brother's love and she didn't have to turn around to know that he had tears in his eyes. She took a deep breath, smiled at Crawford and then looked forward, both at the priest and her future.

CHAPTER 2

"It happened again," Jeff Phillips said to his wife Lauren.

"What happened again?" she asked, pushing her paperwork aside.

"Lily is in her room crying because she witnessed Dylan Mathews getting pushed in class. It's the second time this month. She doesn't understand why the kids in her class are so mean."

"What did you tell her?"

"I tried to explain that it's nothing Dylan did but that the kids who picked on him are unhappy, and that maybe they think pushing Dylan around will make them feel important."

"Is Dylan the little boy who is very overweight?"

Jeff nodded. "That's the one. He's a really cool kid. He's super smart and talented. He played the lead in the school play last Thanksgiving."

Lauren smiled. "I remember him. At Lily's age, I think being smart and talented only gets you the kind of attention you'd rather not have. That's not exactly the message I want to send to our girls. I want our children to be themselves, and if that means being different, then so be it."

"I hear you, but standing out and being different can get you beat up," Jeff added.

Lauren rubbed her pregnant belly and thought about the little boy she was carrying. Early on, they'd made the decision to wait to find out their baby's gender, but after the trauma of her business going up in flames, she changed her mind.

This would be their first boy, and Lauren was very aware of the importance of raising him to be a thoughtful and kind individual, just as they had Olivia and Lily. Yet, she couldn't help feeling concerned about outside influences.

Lauren turned to look at Jeff. "I have a thought."

"Uh-oh, when you say that, it almost always involves me somehow."

"I'm serious, Jeff. What about homeschooling?"

"Homeschooling? How exactly would we accomplish that? I don't know the first thing about homeschooling, and neither do you. Not to mention, it wouldn't be you doing the teaching. It all sounds great until you realize that neither one of us were particularly brilliant in school. You're running a business outside of the home. I'm the stay-at-home dad. You know perfectly well that all of it will fall to me. I don't have a clue how they're doing division these days and forget about algebra and geometry."

"You can do this, Jeff. I'm sure of it. Everyone is doing it and I'm sure we could find out what it entails. You'd be great at this."

Jeff threw his arms in the air. "Don't you dare do that."

"Do what?"

"You know exactly what you're doing. Don't try to sweet-talk me into it. What about what the girls want? Olivia's been in school for seven years, and Lily for almost five. They've got friends in that school. They'll protest. I think it's a mistake. You wait and see."

Lauren turned back to her paperwork and didn't force the issue. Although she hadn't talked to Jeff about it earlier, she'd thought about homeschooling several times in the last month and the reason had nothing to do with schoolyard bullies.

It frustrated her to think that her mother was having more adventures at her age living on Captiva Island than she could offer her children.

Weeks ago when her real estate business burned to the ground, she'd felt the impermanence of life more than ever before. Things had little value to her now and that included their house, car, her business and their retirement accounts. Although she'd found another commercial property, she had little passion for her work.

What did any of those things matter when in the blink of an eye they can all disappear, and there is nothing you can do about it?

She was grateful for her growing family and soon would be on maternity leave from her business, but there was more on her mind than balancing home and work these days.

Thus far, she'd kept her thoughts to herself, but more and more she saw signs that her instincts were right. Her family needed a change, and a drastic one at that.

The Discovery Channel was on the television and when Olivia and Lily came inside from playing with their friends, Lauren insisted they sit and watch what was on.

"Mom, you never want us to watch tv. Why is it ok now?" Olivia asked, sounding more like a teenager every day.

"It's the Discovery Channel, Olivia. There is always something to learn on that channel." Lauren pointed to the screen. "Look, aren't those the cutest Koala bears?"

Lily seemed interested but Olivia played with her new bracelet, totally uninspired by anything on the television.

Lauren rolled her eyes at Jeff. She mouthed, "Do something" to him.

"Olivia, it wouldn't hurt you to learn something about these Koala bears. They're not like other bears, they're special," Jeff said.

Lauren suppressed a laugh. Jeff was trying to get on board with Lauren's desire to educate their children, but he lost Olivia in the first two minutes and had no idea what to do next.

Lauren jumped out of her chair and walked to Olivia and Lily. "Hey, wouldn't you girls love to see these bears in person?"

Lily looked up at her mother and Jeff seemed confused about where Lauren was headed with this line of questioning.

"You mean at the zoo?" Lily asked.

"Well, it's kind of like a zoo. It's in nature, where they're home, climbing trees," Lauren added.

"Are we going to Australia and you forgot to tell me?" Jeff asked, trying to irritate his wife.

"No, we're not going to Australia right now, but maybe in time, we can all go."

"A vacation?" Olivia asked.

Lauren could tell that Jeff was worried she was making a promise she couldn't keep.

"Not right now, Olivia, but soon. Daddy and I need to talk more about it."

Still seeming unimpressed and without looking up, Olivia said matter-of-factly, "Fine, I want the window seat on the plane."

Lauren gave up. If she was going to convince her family to make the kind of move she was thinking about, she'd need to introduce it to them slowly and with conviction.

Nothing in her demeanor today would convince anyone of anything. She'd wait and talk to Jeff when the time was right. Until then, she'd talk to her employees Nell and Brian. Her only concern was how to explain her idea without making them think she'd lost her mind.

———

Beth Walker marched out of her boss' office and slammed the door. She'd finally had enough of his condescending ways and wanted him to see her anger. She was tired of playing the game and felt she'd more than paid her dues. She couldn't demand his respect, nor did she feel that she should have to. She'd earned it every single day on the job and couldn't believe she still had to prove herself.

Frustrated, she didn't know whether to go to her office or leave the building entirely. After a few minutes of seething, she chose the latter.

Slinging the strap of her handbag over her head, she didn't bother to stop at her assistant's desk.

"Um, Beth...I need your signature on these documents," Meredith pleaded as Beth continued to the elevator.

All Beth could do was to raise her hand in the air and not make eye contact. She was afraid of what might come out of her mouth so when the elevator door opened, she got inside and pressed the button for the lobby.

She tipped her head back and let the warm sun hit her face. Taking a deep breath she tried to relax and put the morning's battle behind her. Instead, she focused on the beautiful day and enjoyed the smell of the bakery as she passed the storefront.

Beth had no idea where she was headed, but with a love of the ocean she instinctively walked as close to the harbor as possible.

Working inside the John Joseph Moakley courthouse in the seaport district of Boston was the best part of Beth's job. Every time she looked out the window from her office, she felt a renewed energy to keep up the fight.

However, more and more, the harbor's landscape lost its power to soothe her pain. Dealing with the ugliness of domestic abuse and, in some cases, murder left Beth feeling depressed and hopeless most of the time.

In the Wheeler family, Beth was the one everyone saw as the most optimistic and cheerful. Those days were gone and were now replaced with sleepless nights and constant anxiety.

Her husband Gabriel noticed her changing moods and tried

to encourage her to not let what she couldn't control bother her. As thoughtful and loving as Gabriel tried to be, Beth felt ambivalent. It wasn't as easy as leaving the job to find another. She'd gone through law school and worked tirelessly in a career that she'd once felt a passion for.

She dialed her brother Christopher's cellphone.

"Hey, little brother. Got a minute?"

"Always for you," he answered. "What are you doing calling me in the middle of the day? I thought you'd be busy locking up the bad guys. Is there no one you can have arrested today?" he teased.

"Very funny. How is your day going?"

"No way, you're not going to distract me by making me talk about my job. I can hear it in your voice, sis. What's the matter?"

Finally at Rowes Wharf, Beth sat on a bench and fought back tears.

"I don't know, Chris. I don't think I can do this anymore."

"You're going to have to be more specific. Do what exactly?"

"This job. You remember when I took a leave of absence before? I should have quit then. My gut was telling me that this wasn't the right career path, but I didn't pay attention to how serious things were."

"Beth, listen to me. I know you better than anyone on the planet. You know that."

Beth nodded. Ever since they were children, Christopher was her closest sibling and best friend. It was the reason she called him now.

"Your gut has never failed you. You are strong. If you leave this job it's not because you failed. I know you. That's exactly what you're thinking. But, I'm telling you that's crazy thinking. You can do anything you set your mind to, so if everything in your body is screaming that this isn't the right place for you, then I say, get out. Get out now before it changes you forever. Be Beth Wheeler."

Wiping the tears from her cheek, she said, "You mean Beth Walker, don't you?"

"Nope. Hey, I know you got married. I was at the wedding, remember? No, I *mean* Beth Wheeler. That's who you are deep to the core. Us Wheelers never run from a fight, but sometimes the fight just isn't worth it. Sometimes, you have to walk away because you choose to walk away. You're not running away from anything, my Bethy...and you haven't failed."

Beth felt the weight of her struggles fall away hearing her brother's words. Her family was what gave her strength but it was her brother Christopher who always reminded her of her courage. She needed that now more than ever.

"Thanks, Chris. I needed to hear that. Is it okay if we talk about you and Becca now? Tell me how you guys are doing."

"We're busy as ever. Our schedules are so crazy we barely see each other these days. I guess it's to be expected when you're married to a medical student."

"You two have to squeeze in time now and then for a date night."

Christopher laughed. "Does lunch together in the hospital cafeteria count?"

Beth chuckled. "Well, it will do in a pinch, but I think you need to put a bit more effort into it. I'll talk to Gabriel and see if the four of us can meet in Boston for dinner. It's much easier than Becca and you traveling up north to us. Besides, Boston has so many good restaurants to choose from."

"Sounds like a plan," he said. "In the meantime, what are you going to do about your job?"

Beth sighed. "Right now, I'm going to go back to my desk and finish the paperwork I've been putting off. After that, I'm not sure."

"Well, whatever you do. Make sure it's your decision and no one else's. If all else fails there's always a call to Mom."

Beth rolled her eyes and laughed at the suggestion. "I'm

grateful at the moment she's across the Atlantic enjoying Italy with Paolo. If she was still in Florida, I'd probably be on the next flight to Captiva to have one of her special talks with a cup of her tea. I'm surprised Becca could get away to Italy to be in the wedding. Why didn't you go with her?"

"She went just for the wedding and is flying back right after it's over. It didn't make sense to spend the money quite frankly. The way she explained it to me was that she couldn't miss her dad's wedding but she'll pay for it when she returns, trying to catch up. I know it meant the world to her to go, so I understand."

Clouds covered the sun and the sky looked like it was going to suddenly rain.

"I better get back to the office. Thanks, Chris. I mean it. You always know how to make me feel better."

"Hang in there. You'll know what to do when the time is right. I'll talk to Becca about us getting together. Love you, Bethy."

"Love you too."

CHAPTER 3

*M*aggie brushed the hair from her daughter Sarah's face.

"You looked beautiful up there at the altar. It reminded me of your wedding to Trevor."

"Thanks, Mom. I'm just so thrilled that Trevor finally agreed to leave work long enough for our family to see Italy for the first time."

"When will you leave Gaeta?" Maggie asked.

"Day after tomorrow. Did I tell you that Emma Thurston is meeting us in Rome? She's been on assignment in Paris but could get a few days off so we could get some time together."

"Oh, Sarah, that's wonderful. I always liked Emma." Maggie looked over at Emma's sister Jillian. Nodding in her direction, she said, "I see her sister Jillian is still dating Crawford's son, Finn. They look cozy enough. Any word on how that's going?"

Sarah shook her head. "I'm in the dark on that. It's possible Ciara knows more and I'm sure that Emma doesn't know anything either. She's been so busy lately, I don't think she's had time to talk with her family at all. I asked Jillian if she was going to see her sister on this trip, but she said that she and Finn were flying back tomorrow."

Maggie and Sarah laughed at Chelsea who was dancing with a very handsome Italian man.

"I don't think she's missed a dance yet," Sarah said.

"She's going to have a heart attack if she doesn't slow down. She's on a statin and high blood pressure medicine."

Maggie waved to Chelsea to come join her and Sarah. Fanning herself with a fan from the local gift shop, Chelsea plopped onto a chair next to Maggie.

"Holy cow, is it me or is Italy really hot?"

Maggie chuckled. Pushing a glass toward Chelsea, she said, "I think it's a bit of both. Have some water and stay hydrated."

"Did you see the guy I was dancing with?"

"Which one? You've danced with half the town."

"The last one. He's a distant cousin. I think maybe his mother and Paolo's mother were second cousins. Anyway, he's family but he doesn't live in Gaeta. He lives in Florence and has a jewelry store. He was telling me all about the amount of jewelry, especially gold, that the tourists buy. He said his brother, who still lives here in Gaeta, owns the pizza place near where we're staying."

"Trevor and I ate there yesterday. The pizza is amazing. They don't cut it in triangles the way we do back home. These pizzas were square and thick but full of flavor. Trevor had three pieces and we both agreed that it's the sauce that makes it so delicious."

"Well, anyway, his name is Antonio and his brother is Aldo," Chelsea continued. "Antonio invited all of us to go to Florence after the wedding."

"Paolo and I are flying home in two days. I think Florence is out for us, but you should go," Maggie said.

Chelsea shook her head. "No, I'm going home with you all. Florence will have to wait for another time." Chelsea looked at

Sarah, "What about you and your family? I hear you plan to make a vacation out of this visit to Italy."

Sarah nodded. "Yup. We're headed to Rome and then Venice. We'll stay another week and then get back. Trevor's been working so hard and I know he's still a little anxious leaving the company in his brothers' hands. He called home around four o'clock this morning Italy time to see how his father's doing. I guess he's healing and is pushing to get back to work."

"Isn't it too soon after his stroke?" Maggie asked.

"Trevor thinks it is, not just because of the workload, but because there are still unresolved issues between Devon and his son Wyatt. Trevor was a little nervous about letting Wyatt back into the company, but I think he's overreacting. I guess time will tell."

Ciara and Crawford approached them carrying a tray of champagne. "Come on you guys, time for a refresher."

"Not for me, thank you. I think I'm refreshed enough," Maggie said. "Any more and I'll refresh myself right to sleep."

Paolo stepped in front of Maggie and bowed. "May I have this dance?"

"I thought you'd never ask," Maggie said, taking her husband's hand. She looked back at her friends. "Excuse me but this handsome man needs my attention."

As they moved toward the middle of the dance floor, Paolo placed his hand on Maggie's back and began to sing the words to the Italian love song, Al Di La.

"I've never heard you sing before," she said. "You have a beautiful voice. Promise me that when we get back to Captiva, you'll keep singing."

He shook his head. "Nope, I only sing in Italian. I don't think any of our guests want to hear me sing."

Maggie smiled. "On the contrary. I think once they hear you, we'll need to hire musicians and make live music a regular thing at the inn."

Paolo pulled her closer. "I'll make you a promise. If you make my mother's recipe for lasagna, I'll continue to sing love songs, but only to you."

Maggie laughed. "You've got a deal."

They danced two more slow songs before the crowd of mostly young kids jumped onto the dance floor when the faster music began.

"I think this is our cue to sit."

They walked back to Sarah who'd been joined by her husband Trevor.

"Where's Chelsea?" Maggie asked.

Sarah pointed to the dance floor.

Maggie rolled her eyes. "Here we go again."

<hr>

Jillian Thurston pulled Finn Powell off the dance floor. "I need a break. My feet are killing me," she said. "That's what I get for dancing in new heels," she said as she pulled her shoes off and threw them under the table.

"I've had enough champagne, too. Maybe it's time for one of those bottled waters."

Finn jumped up and grabbed two bottles of water from the ice bucket.

"Looks like you're not the only one taking your shoes off," Finn said, pointing to Chelsea.

Jillian laughed. "Wow, I guess not. Forget about the shoes, I hope I'm out there dancing when I'm her age."

"She's not that old, Jill. I mean I'm pretty sure she's close to my father's age."

"I didn't mean anything by it. I'm just saying that I love how Chelsea embraces life and she doesn't let anything stop her. I admire that, don't you?"

Finn nodded. "I do. I think it's great no matter your age that you have passion in your life."

Her face serious, Jillian could tell that he was directing their conversation to a more personal subject. "Passion? Who said anything about passion?"

Finn blushed. "Um, I thought that's what we were talking about."

She smiled. "I'm only teasing you. Yes, passion is what drives us I guess."

Finn shrugged. "I'm not sure that's exactly right. I've heard that humans are very predictable because their behavior, decisions, and purpose...most emotions for that matter are driven by our need to either go towards pleasure or run away from pain. I suppose the more pleasurable, the easier and faster the drive in that direction."

Jillian admired Finn's philosophical point of view. "Is that how you see human behavior?"

"I'm not sure. I have thought about it though and even measured that thinking against my own actions. For instance, right now, I want to kiss you. My decision on whether to do so might ultimately be influenced by my fear of rejection. I would need to decide whether that pain outweighs my need for the feeling of pleasure I'd receive from your lips."

She tried not to laugh, keeping her composure and an introspective face. "I see what you mean. I suppose knowing you as well as I do, I can predict what you'll do in this situation."

He leaned in closer to hear her answer. "Yes?"

"I'm going to say no. No to the kiss but thank you."

Disappointment registered on Finn's face. "No kiss?"

Jillian shook her head. "No kiss. But I do have a question for you. Just for the sake of education, what happens to that human when he gets rejected? I mean, you haven't followed through with your supposition. You need to study this further, don't you think?"

"How so?"

"Well, you didn't answer my question. What happens to the human after he suffers pain? Will he avoid that situation in the future? Let's take the kiss for example. You've been rebuffed. Do you slither away and learn not to ask for another kiss, or do you try again?"

Finn sat back and pretended to ponder the question. Jillian was pleased with the way she'd handled the situation, but was shocked when Finn bent down, pulled her into his arms and kissed her deeply and for almost a minute. When he pulled away from her, he smiled and said, "You forgot about passion. Passion always outweighs rejection. You could rebuff me one hundred times, Jillian Thurston, but I'll always keep asking."

She wanted to respond but he wouldn't let her. As he kissed her again, her heart skipped a beat as she fell in love with Finn Powell once more.

Across the room, Crawford and Ciara held each other close and watched everyone enjoying the celebration.

"Did you see that?" Crawford asked his bride.

Ciara smiled. "You mean did I see your son kiss his girlfriend? Yes, I did. What's so unusual about that?"

"It wasn't that he kissed her. It was the way he kissed her. I think that boy is in love. Has he said anything to you?"

Ciara shook her head. "Crawford, I doubt that Finn is going to talk to me about his feelings for Jillian."

Becca joined them. "Are you two seeing what I'm seeing?"

"Your brother is in love," Crawford answered. "Perhaps we all should stop staring at them. He's going to be embarrassed if we keep this up."

Crawford turned to his daughter and kissed her forehead.

"I'm so happy you were able to come to the wedding. It means the world to both of us. I only wish Chris could have made it."

"I know, Dad, but honestly, it would have been too much for him. Because of my school and work, he doesn't complain about his job or the responsibilities he has on his shoulders to make the place a success. Channel 5 was coming to Summit to film the work he's been doing with the kids. There was no way he could reschedule that."

Ciara kissed Becca's cheek. "Thank you for being a bridesmaid. You and Sarah made this day extra special."

"I was so happy you asked me, Ciara. You and Dad make a wonderful couple. I hate to party and run, but I've got to pack. I've got a red-eye flight back to Boston. Congratulations again and have a wonderful Italian honeymoon. I've got to find Joshua and Luke to say goodbye. I guess I'll start with Finn if I can pry him away from Jillian for two seconds."

"Safe travels, honey," Crawford said. "When you and Chris can get even a couple of days off, come down to Captiva for a visit. We miss you both."

The sun was about to set and the reception's small twinkling white lights illuminated the entire town square. As the wine flowed and the cake passed to the guests, Ciara turned to Crawford, and wrapped her arms around his neck. They swayed to the music as Crawford leaned down to kiss his wife.

"I think it's time you and I begin our honeymoon. Let's let everyone enjoy the rest of the evening. You and I have a private party of our own to attend."

Ciara smiled as Crawford took her hand and led her away from the crowd down the street to their own bed & breakfast overlooking the Mediterranean Sea.

CHAPTER 4

*O*n her rare day off, Riley Cuthbert loved to swim in the ocean and spend the day doing as little as possible. That was her plan until Millie raved about a restaurant she'd visited two days earlier on Sanibel Island. Intrigued by the menu, she decided to give up her beach day and drive to Sanibel to check it out.

As Senior Chef at the Key Lime Garden Inn, Riley loved to search for new menu ideas. Always careful not to copy another chef's creation, she'd find ways to make it her own by changing out an ingredient or two.

When she reached The Pelican Porch, a young woman approached and asked Riley to follow her to a single table nearest to the garden.

The restaurant was a lovely mix of Caribbean colors and an island open-air dining area and a wrap-around porch with smaller tables for two. Each table was designed with seashells and tea lights and the smells coming from the kitchen were heavenly.

"Thank you, "Riley said as the woman handed her a menu.

"Can I get you something to drink?" the woman asked.

"Iced tea please."

"I'll be right back."

When the waitress returned with her iced tea, Riley chose the seared scallops and brussels sprouts over parsnip puree for her lunch.

There were plenty of empty tables which concerned Riley given the time of day. Almost all restaurants on both Sanibel and Captiva were filled at lunch time. Millie raved about the food and so Riley didn't worry.

Shocked when a man fell into the other chair at her table, Riley looked around to see if anyone witnessed the intrusion.

"Smile and act like we're good friends. I'll say something and then you laugh," he said.

Stunned, all she could say was, "What?"

"Please, you'll save my life if you just go along with me on this. Do you see a woman at the front door? Red hair, large colorful beach bag on her arm?"

Riley nodded. "She's obsessed with me and won't leave me alone. If she thinks I'm with someone, she'll go away. Please, I'll pay you...just act like we're close."

"How much?" Riley asked.

"How much, what?"

"How much will you pay me?"

"Oh, for heaven's sake...fine, twenty dollars."

"Fifty, and she's coming over here," she added to put additional pressure on him.

"Fine, fifty dollars."

Riley put her hand on his and smiled. He reached across the table and touched her face.

"Hello, Andrew," the woman said, not taking her eyes off Riley.

He turned to look at her and nodded. "Hello, Gwen. Nice to see you. This is my girlfriend..."

"Riley." Riley finished his sentence while extending her hand to the woman.

He repeated her name. "Yes, Riley."

"Gwen Bradford, nice to meet you. I suppose Andrew never mentioned me?"

Riley shook her head. "No. He never did."

"Well, I was his girlfriend before you," she responded.

Andrew shook his head. "To be fair, Gwen, we only had one date. That doesn't exactly make you my girlfriend."

"Whatever," Gwen answered.

The waitress brought Riley's lunch. The fact that there was only one plate made the situation all the more awkward.

"Andrew, you're not eating?" Gwen asked.

"No, I'm not hungry. Listen, Gwen, Riley and I would like to be alone. I hope you'll understand. It was nice to see you again and I wish you well, but I'm in a committed relationship now and I'd like us to leave things on a positive note."

Riley thought the situation comical, but she hoped the woman wasn't dangerous.

"It was nice to meet you, Riley. Enjoy your lunch. Goodbye, Andrew."

Andrew nodded. "Take care, Gwen."

Riley watched the woman walk out of the restaurant and get into a car.

"Is she gone?" he asked, not wanting to turn around.

"Yup. You're good to leave now, yourself. I'd like to eat my lunch if it's all the same to you."

He got up from the table. "Thanks for the help. I'm sorry if I disturbed you."

He started to walk away when Riley yelled to him, "Um, not so fast. You owe me fifty dollars."

He sat back across from her. "I tell you what, how about I take you out to dinner instead. I have pretty good taste in food. I mean, I come here often and the food is great so you can trust me on this."

Riley couldn't deny his jet black hair and ocean-blue eyes were hard to resist. Nonetheless, she didn't know anything about this guy who had a crazy woman following him.

"That remains to be seen. I haven't even taken one bite yet. It looks good but looks can be deceiving."

His smile was as gorgeous as the rest of him.

"Why don't you take a few bites and if you think the food is good, say you'll let me take you to dinner?"

She took a few bites of the scallops and was surprised at how they practically melted in her mouth. The brussels sprouts were equally satisfying.

"Well?" he asked.

Riley smiled and nodded. "Okay, I'll give you this one. I'll agree to one dinner, and one dinner only because you owe me fifty bucks."

"Great." He pulled out a piece of paper and handed it to her. "Write down your name, number and address and I'll pick you up tomorrow night at seven if that works for you."

Shocked at herself for going along with this, she took the paper and wrote her information on it. She handed it back to him and he read her name aloud. "Riley Cuthbert. It's nice to meet you, Riley, but I've got to get back to work. I'm glad you like my cooking."

With that, he walked away and into the kitchen.

I can't believe this. He's the chef?

She wanted to laugh but instead thought the best course of action was to eat every last drop of food on the plate. It was the only way she could let him know that she approved of not only the food, but of him as well.

If this was their first encounter, Riley couldn't wait for their first date.

"Do you ever get the feeling that people think there's something wrong if you're middle aged and not married?" Millie asked Linda St. James as they walked the beach trying to get ten thousand steps on their smart watches.

"All the time," Linda answered. "I don't let it get to me though. I mean, think about it. Does anyone call Diane Keaton an old maid?"

"I hadn't thought of it like that," Millie answered between breaths.

"So, how's it going at the inn? When do Maggie and Chelsea get back?" Linda asked.

"Should be tomorrow, and I don't mind telling you that I can't wait."

"Oh? Trouble at the inn?" Linda asked, always looking for gossip.

"No, nothing like that. It's been a lot of work to run things with just Riley, Iris and me. It's not the cleaning or doing the books that's the problem, it's really the garden. I don't know a thing about gardening. All I'm focused on is keeping things watered. That's probably the most important."

"Well, yeah, that and not letting the plants die," Linda said. "Anyway, what's got you talking about being single? Has someone said something to you?"

"No, it's just that I feel like everyone around me is either in love or getting married. I mean those things are nice for some people but it's not for me. I didn't know this about myself until recently. I've gone on dates but I've turned down more offers than I've accepted. I like not having to check in with someone about what I'm doing."

"I know what you mean. Although, I was sort of smitten with Crawford Powell for a bit. I helped out a lot at his house after Julia died."

"You were? I didn't know that."

"It's no big deal. Ciara is the right woman for him. I'm glad they got married. She's a lovely person and he deserves to be happy."

"I do have moments of regret though. You know how it is. I was married to a real jerk and so my perspective is probably skewed towards not trusting men. I can see how wonderful marriage can be when both parties are on the same page. I just wasn't lucky in that way, and now that I've been alone a while, I really like it," Millie explained.

"I'm with you. Relationships can be trouble. I think you and I should form a club."

"A club?"

"Yeah, you know, a club of single women who want to stay single and don't want a man in their life. That kind of club," Linda said.

Suddenly, Millie realized that her commitment to the life she'd chosen was more personal than she'd thought. She had no problem admitting to Linda that she was happy being single, but announcing it felt more like she was walking around with a man-repellent sign.

"Oh, I don't know. I'm not sure a club is the right way to go with this. It's just a feeling after all," Millie said.

"Millicent Brenner, you either really mean what you say or you don't, which is it?"

Millie didn't like Linda's tone, and there seemed something militant about this club she was forming in her head.

"Linda, why don't we just sit on this for a while. I mean, what happens if some really nice man comes into your life? Are you going to tell him to go away?"

Linda thought about that for a minute. "Well, I don't know."

"Exactly. I think we should keep our options open," Millie explained.

"I suppose you have a point. We should definitely stay open-minded about this. Let's make a pact. If Mr. Wonderful comes around we'll give him a chance, but if he doesn't, we're fine with that too."

Millie nodded. "That sounds right to me." She looked at her smart watch. "We've got three thousand more steps to go. Should we get back to it?"

Linda shrugged. "Nah, I think we've done enough for today."

"How many steps did we do?" Millie asked.

"Two thousand eight hundred," Linda answered.

They both nodded. No one said a word for a few minutes until Linda had an idea. "Want to go to the Bubble Room for one of their cakes?"

"Oh, that sounds great. I suppose we have to walk there?"

"Nope. I left my golf cart right in front of The Mucky Duck. Let's go."

CHAPTER 5

"*V*uoi che ti faccia una foto?…you like me to take your picture?" the man asked Sarah as she, Trevor and their children stood in front of the Colosseum.

"Oh yes, would you? Thank you so much."

"Everyone say parmiggiano!" Trevor said.

"Parmiggiano!" all but little Maggie yelled.

"Grazie," Sarah said to the man.

"Di Niente," he answered.

"What did he say, Mama?" Sophia asked.

"He said 'you're welcome.'"

"When did you learn Italian?" Trevor asked.

"I studied a few things before we left. I thought it might come in handy."

"By any chance, did you learn how to ask where the closest gelato place is?"

Sarah laughed. "I missed that lesson. I'm sure we can find one around here somewhere. Maggie looks ready for a nap, are you sure we shouldn't go back to the hotel?"

"Maybe you're right. How much time do we have before you have to meet Emma?"

"Only an hour. I think what we should do is go back to the hotel and order gelato there. I saw it on the menu. That way the kids can relax, Maggie can take her nap and maybe later we all can go swimming in the hotel pool."

"I want to go in the pool," Noah said.

Looking at her cellphone, Sarah added, "I'm meeting Emma in front of the Trevi Fountain and looking at my GPS; it's not that far from our hotel. I should be able to walk there."

"Sounds good. Let's go. Noah, take my hand, the traffic is crazy here."

Cars raced around the city and Sarah worried that walking with the kids might have been a mistake. "Do you think we need a taxi?"

"No, it's not really that far. Besides, we don't have car seats for the kids. It's only a few more blocks. Stay close and on the sidewalk."

Sarah held Maggie tight and walked close behind Trevor who was carrying Sophia and holding Noah's hand. As beautiful as Rome was, Sarah enjoyed the quiet of Gaeta and the absence of speeding automobiles.

When they finally reached the hotel, there was a collective sigh of relief.

"Am I crazy or was the only thing keeping us from getting run over two quick beeps of a Fiat? I mean, do these drivers really think that's their only responsibility so they don't run over tourists?"

Sarah's nervous laugh did little to calm Trevor's outrage. "I'm not sure I want you to walk to meet Emma."

"I'll be fine," she insisted.

They got off the elevator and Noah pulled on Trevor's arm. "Daddy, you said we can get ice cream."

Sarah laughed. "Not even the threat of being hit by a car in the middle of Rome can stop a child's memory of a promised gelato."

"What did I tell you about patience, Noah? Can you see that

Maggie is asleep? Let's get her in bed and then we'll order the ice cream."

Sarah watched as Noah sat on his bed, pouting.

"I feel bad leaving you. I think you might have your hands full with an unhappy boy."

"He'll get over it," Trevor whispered as he walked Sarah to the door. "Listen, text me when you get there so I don't worry."

"I will," she said. They kissed and she walked toward the elevator.

"Say hello to Emma and tell her to get back to Captiva soon," he added.

Following her GPS, Sarah walked several blocks toward Piccolo Buco. When the restaurant was within view she could see Emma waving near the front door.

"Hey, you made it," Emma said as she wrapped her arms around Sarah.

"I can't believe that I'm actually in Rome," Sarah said.

She stepped back to look at her best friend. "You look incredible."

"Oh, stop. I look like I always do."

"No, I mean it. Something is different," Sarah insisted.

Emma held up her left hand and wiggled her ring finger. "Maybe it's this wedding band."

"What? No way. You didn't! You got married?"

Emma laughed. "I did. Two weeks ago in Verona. I would have waited for you but Gareth wanted to do it right away. Can you believe it? I haven't told anyone, not even my family."

Sarah pulled Emma inside. "Let's get a table so you can tell me everything."

They were led to a table toward the back of the restaurant and quickly ordered two coffees.

"I'm sorry, but I'm in complete shock about this," Sarah said.

"You? Imagine how I feel. I was absolutely certain that I'd never get married. I mean, after Timothy died, I never even thought I'd fall in love again, let alone say 'I do.'"

"How did this happen?"

Emma laughed. "Well, Gareth had flown to Milan for a meeting, I was on assignment in Padua. Neither of us had ever been to Verona and I had a few days off. The next thing I know we're standing under Juliet's balcony and he gets down on one knee."

"Oh, wow. That's so romantic."

"I didn't know what to think. At first, I thought he was making a joke…you know, acting like Romeo. He was quoting Shakespeare for heaven's sake. When I realized that he wasn't kidding, I stood there frozen in place. There were tons of people there because…well, you know, it's Juliet's balcony. I think everyone saw what was going on before I did."

Looking at Emma's left hand, Sarah could only see a single gold band. "Where's the ring? Did he have a ring when he proposed?"

Emma shook her head. "No ring. You know me, Sarah. That's not my style. I'm a plain gold band kind of girl. With my job I can't really afford to wear a diamond ring anyway."

"What do you mean?"

"Well, I've been in some dicey situations. I've told you this before."

Sarah shrugged, "I know, but how can your ring be a problem?"

Emma's face turned serious and her voice was only a whisper.

"I had nothing of value on me when Timothy was shot. If I had something…anything to offer the terrorists to save him…."

Sarah reached across the table and placed her hand on Emma's. "Oh, honey, I know that. You and I both know there was nothing you could do."

Looking down at her hand, Emma nodded. "I know. It's just

that if I were ever to wear a diamond, I'd immediately think of Timothy and I can't have that image in my head. You know?"

Sarah nodded. "Of course."

Emma suddenly sat up in her chair and smiled. "Anyway, the deed is done. I'm a married lady now."

The tension shifted to happier times.

"I'm so happy for you. But where is your groom? I thought Gareth was going to be here."

"That was the plan, but he had to return to New York to meet with his editor. He's working on a new book and he has deadlines. He told me to apologize and let you know that he'll see you in a couple of weeks."

"A couple of weeks? Where? When?"

"We're going to Florida. I can't put off telling my family. I'm going to stop and see Jillian first and convince her to come with us. I need moral support."

Sarah's face lit up and she took a sip of her espresso. Trying not to giggle, she shook her head.

"What's so funny?"

"You, telling your parents that you're married. I'd love to be a fly on that wall. Anyway, I'm glad you're coming. This coffee is amazing, but we need to celebrate. When you get home give me a call. We're going to need champagne...and lots of it."

When Maggie and Paolo returned home from Italy, Paolo immediately resumed work on the tiny cottage and cabana at the end of their property line.

Maggie couldn't wait to wiggle her toes in the Captiva sand once more. She extended her arms and reached for the sky. She was home and not even the beauty of Italy could replace the joy she felt for her beloved Captiva Island.

She turned back and walked to where Paolo was working.

"Are you glad to be home?" she asked.

Carrying several two by fours and dropping them onto a pile of lumber, he shrugged. "Yes and no. The whole time we were in Gaeta, I kept thinking about this project. Now that we're home, I keep thinking of Italy." He pulled the scarf from his neck and wiped his face. "I'm sure it's the Florida heat that's got me struggling."

Maggie laughed. "Well, I've got a cure for what ails you. I'll bring down some lemonade if you promise to stop working long enough to go to the animal shelter. Remember, you promised?"

"Oh, Maggie, really? Can't that wait until this job is done?"

Disappointed, Maggie frowned. "You promised. How many times are we going to put this off? Do you want a dog or not?"

She cringed at the stupidity of asking that question considering that he might have changed his mind.

Paolo stopped working and didn't say anything for a few seconds. He wiped his face again and stared at her. "Does it really matter what I think? The look you're giving me pretty much says we're getting a puppy."

Her smile back again, Maggie shrugged. "Well, I don't know about that. I'm not sure what we'll get. The way I look at it, I think it's the dog that picks the human."

Paolo nodded. "Yes, I've heard that too. What time do I have to be ready to meet my owner?"

Maggie laughed. "I hope it's a girl. You can never say no to a woman."

The sign read "No-Kill Animal Shelter."

"How long do you keep the dogs? I mean, what if no one ever picks them? Do you still care for them?" Maggie asked the woman holding an adorable Yorkshire Terrier.

"We do, indeed. This little guy was here for six months before someone took him home," she answered.

Confused, Paolo asked the obvious question. "I guess the fact that he's here means they brought him back?"

The woman laughed at Paolo's question.

"Not quite. I adopted him. His name is Tucker, and he's pretty much the shelter's mascot."

Maggie and Paolo rubbed the pup's mane. "Hello, Tucker. You are adorable. Let's see if we can find a pup as sweet as you to come home with us."

"I'm Kristin, nice to meet you both. Follow me to the back and let's see if you might find a new friend."

Excited and nervous, Maggie squeezed Paolo's arm. Several cages to the right and left were occupied and the tug at Maggie's heart was strong.

"My goodness, I want to take them all home."

Kristen's face looked sad. "Almost everyone who comes here says that. It's hard to meet each one and then walk away. If it helps you at all, know that we take very good care of these pups. You could say that we spoil them as much as possible."

Maggie could tell that Kristen loved the animals and was happy to know that her dog would have been loved and cared for before coming home to the Key Lime Garden Inn.

"Hey, what's going on, little one?" Paolo said as he turned to see who was hitting his leg.

"That's Lexi. She's a chihuahua. Her owner just passed away. Lexi is only two years old and her owner got her when she was born. Unfortunately, the woman had cancer and couldn't find anyone to take Lexi. It's so sad because we could tell when she brought Lexi to us that she didn't want to give her up. I promised her that we'd find Lexi a good home and would take care of her until we did."

"Can I hold her?" Paolo asked.

Maggie had tears in her eyes not only because of Lexi's situation but that her husband had already fallen in love with the little girl.

Maggie knew that she would have to handle the paperwork, donation and whatever other formalities were necessary because Paolo and their new family member were enjoying a spoonful of peanut butter together.

When she was done, Maggie watched her husband explain to Lexi what it meant to have a forever home. Having already found her place in the world, Maggie understood exactly how important that was. Nothing felt as wonderful as knowing where you belong. Even if where you came from wasn't all that perfect.

CHAPTER 6

*R*iley's eyes were wide with both excitement and shock. Andrew walked into the Key Lime Garden Inn and made his way into the kitchen. He knocked on the open door and smiled.

"I followed voices," he said, his smile broadening by the second.

"Can I help you?" Maggie asked.

"I'm here to see Riley Cuthbert," he answered.

Maggie looked at Riley and then back at the man.

Riley took her apron off, placed it on the counter and came out from behind the kitchen island.

"Maggie, this is Andrew…" She suddenly realized she didn't know his last name.

"Hansen," he said.

Riley smiled and nodded. "Andrew Hansen. He's the chef at The Plover Porch restaurant in Sanibel."

Andrew extended his hand to Maggie. "The Pelican Porch," he corrected Riley.

Riley wanted the floor to gobble her up and never let her see the light of day again.

The awkward moment led Maggie to excuse herself. "Nice to meet you, Mr. Hansen. I've got paperwork in my office if you'll excuse me."

He nodded and as Maggie walked out of the room, Riley grabbed his arm, pulling him into the dining room.

"What are you doing here?"

"Looking for you obviously. I couldn't wait until tonight."

His smile, although distracting, irritated more than charmed her. "I never said where I worked. All you had was my name and my number. Explain yourself."

He leaned against the frame of the front door and crossed his arms. "Is it possible that you don't know how famous you are? It didn't take me long to find out that you are one of the most celebrated chefs in Florida."

"What?"

"You mean you've never Googled yourself? Come on, that's not possible."

"Mr. Hansen, I don't know what you're trying to do here, but I don't like being stalked."

"Technically, I'm not stalking you. You gave me your name and number and made a date with me. At least, that's how the police would see it I'm sure."

"I can fix that." Riley opened the front door. "I'm calling off our date and I'd like you to leave."

He hesitated but when he saw that she was serious, he nodded his head and walked out the door. He started for his car but stopped and turned to look at her.

"I'm really sorry, Riley. I was so excited for our date tonight, I couldn't wait to see you. When I found out that you were a chef at the Key Lime Garden Inn I had to see your kitchen. I'm truly sorry if I was disrespectful in any way. I hope you believe me."

She didn't want to admit that she was flattered by all the attention and that he had gone to such lengths to track her down. Still, she needed to take control of the situation.

Softening, she moved toward him and extended her hand. "Why don't we start over? I'd say our second encounter was just as unorthodox as our first. Let's let that not happen a third time."

Looking relieved, he smiled once again and took her hand. "Thank you for taking pity on me. Can I be so bold as to assume we're still on for tonight?"

"Let's give it another try. Now that you know where I work, how about you meet me here at seven?"

Still holding her hand he didn't let go until she did.

"Okay, see you at seven," he said as he walked down the stairs and got into his car.

Riley closed the door and leaned against it.

"Was that Andrew Hansen?" Millie asked, carrying sheets to the laundry room. Maggie joined them in the hall.

Riley was surprised that Millie knew Andrew.

"Yes, how do you know him?"

"I don't really, only what I've read about him, and of course, I've eaten at his restaurant. I told you about him."

"You told me to check out the food, which I did. You never said anything about him specifically."

"Is Andrew famous or something? Why all the fuss?" Maggie asked.

"Oh, he's famous all right. Did you know he was in that magazine as one of the sexiest bachelors of 2021?"

Riley walked back into the kitchen with Millie and Maggie following her. Iris was in the dining room preparing it for the dinner guests.

Trying to keep her feelings to herself, Riley wanted everyone to stop talking about her date. Before long, they'd be asking her questions she didn't want to answer.

"He's coming back, right?" Maggie asked.

"Yes, he'll be here at seven. I'm having him pick me up here. Is that okay with you? I mean, I've brought a change of clothes and not all the rooms are booked. I thought maybe I could take a shower and..."

"Not another word. Of course you can. The inn is your home. Besides, I want another look at this Andrew. He better treat you right or Paolo will make him wish he had."

Millie looked like she was going to faint.

"Millie are you all right?" Maggie asked.

Millie nodded. "I'm fine. I just can't believe that a 2021 sexiest bachelor is going to be here tonight. Wait until I tell Linda."

Riley panicked. "Oh, Millie, please don't pass this around, especially to that woman. She's the biggest gossip on the island. Before you know it, there'll be tons of women descending on the inn when Andrew gets here."

Millie now looked disappointed. Since moving to Captiva, Linda St. James had become her best friend. She hated not being able to tell her about Andrew.

However, she had an idea. She could wait until the last minute, and then drag Linda to the inn. Her friend would be forever grateful when Millie told her what the mystery was all about. Riley couldn't possibly complain about Linda visiting her best friend at work.

Grinning from ear to ear, Millie quickly finished doing the laundry and whatever chores remained. She'd be ready with camera in hand when Andrew arrived. If all went well, she'd spend the night at Linda's and talk till the early morning hours about Captiva's newest romance.

Lauren waited until Nell and Brian were finished with their phone calls before she interrupted them.

"Hey, guys, can you all come into the conference room? I'd like to talk to the two of you about something."

"Sure," Nell answered, and then looked at Brian.

"Yeah, of course," he said.

Pacing the room, Lauren spoke first.

"I know things have been crazy around here with all the changes. I really appreciate how the two of you have stepped up to help me get this place up and running."

"You've been through a lot, Lauren," Nell said.

"I'm not the only one. Both of you have had to adjust as well."

"I feel like things are finally getting back to normal, though, don't you?" Brian asked.

"Oh, for sure. New clients have come in. We're making money. The office is better than the one we lost in the fire."

Lauren sat and tried to think of how best to explain what had been on her mind these last few weeks. Not wanting to give anything away, she chose her words carefully.

"I just wanted to give you a heads up about something I've been thinking about. My family and I are struggling to find a happy balance with the girls and school. With the baby coming and my pregnancy leave, I'm not sure how long I'll be gone. I know I said I'd only take about six weeks, but it's possible it might be longer."

"How much longer are you thinking?" Nell asked.

Lauren smiled and shrugged. "Oh, I don't know...maybe... um...forever."

Brian was the first to catch on.

"You're closing the business down?"

"Oh, Lauren, no...you can't. You've worked so hard to make this place a success. What does Jeff say about it?"

Nell's question was the proverbial elephant in the room.

"I haven't told him yet."

"What? Who have you told?"

Lauren's nervous laugh said everything. "Just you two...for now."

The shocked look on Nell and Brian's faces convinced Lauren to say more.

"Hear me out. I'm not sure that I want to sell. I know how much the two of you love it here, and you're the best at what you do. I haven't crunched the numbers yet, and of course I'll run it by my accountant, but maybe I can let the two of you run the place in my extended absence."

"You think you can afford that?" Nell asked.

Brian looked at Nell. "I don't know about you, but if Lauren does decide to sell, what do you think about the two of us buying the business?"

Lauren smiled. She didn't want to suggest that possibility and was thrilled when Brian brought it up.

"Who, us? Go into business together? We'd kill each other," Nell insisted.

"No, you wouldn't. I've watched the two of you work together on projects a million times. You negotiate well. You communicate well and even when you disagree one of you always gives in."

"Yeah, it's usually me," Brian teased.

"Listen, let's not get the cart before the horse here. I don't know what I'm going to do, but I thought it best to bring this to your attention just as soon as possible. You both need to really think about this, and so do I."

They all got up from their chairs and Nell hugged Lauren. "Whatever you decide, we'll support you."

"Absolutely," Brian added. "By the way, I never pictured you as a stay at home mom. Is that really what you want to do?"

Lauren smiled. "Nope. I was thinking more like hiking in the Amazon Rainforest."

They all laughed, but it was Lauren who knew that she was only half joking.

Beth stood before her husband and dangled her car keys.

"I've been looking everywhere for my keys. Guess where they were?"

Gabriel put his cellphone down on the sofa and looked up at her.

"The refrigerator. My keys were right next to the oat milk. I swear I'm losing my mind. Yesterday, I shrunk two blouses that were dry-clean only. I've had them for years and I always remember to keep them out of the washing machine. Now, I've got to throw them away. Where is my mind?"

"If I had to guess, it's because you're putting off something that you don't want to do."

Beth sat next to Gabriel and rested her head on his shoulder. "How come you're so smart?"

Gabriel laughed. "Can I quote you in the future when you tell me I'm wrong about something?"

She sat up and turned to him. "No, you cannot. I'm having a moment of ambivalence. You can't take advantage of that."

Gabriel put his arm around her and pulled her back. "Maybe when you don't know what to do, you shouldn't do anything."

Beth settled into the safety and comfort of his arms and closed her eyes. "Good idea. I say we don't go to work today and we stay right here on this sofa."

"I have a better idea," he responded. "How about I go to work and you call your mother?"

"My mother?"

"Why not? As long as I've known you, whenever you're struggling with something, she seems to know exactly what to say to you. I'd like to claim that power, but you and your mother are on a whole different level."

There was silence for a minute before Beth answered him. "I'm not ready."

"Huh? What do you mean?"

She sat up straight and looked him in the eye. "My mother has a way of getting to the heart of the matter within five minutes of listening to me. I'm not sure that I'm ready to hear what she has to say."

Gabriel smiled. "What you mean is that you're not ready to follow through with quitting your job."

She bent down and patted their dog Charlie's head.

"I know it's what I have to do, but I was hoping that I'd have a plan for what I'll do after I leave before I pull the plug. You know how people say when a door closes, a window opens somewhere? I just can't see beyond the end of my nose right now…and that scares me. I know I'll call my mother when I'm ready."

Beth kissed Gabriel's cheek. "I better get to work. Whatever I decide, I've still got bills to pay."

CHAPTER 7

*F*eeling she'd over-reacted to Andrew's visit to the Key Lime Garden Inn, Riley reminded herself to lighten up and not spend the evening looking for signs that the date was a mistake.

Since the moment Andrew sat across from her at his restaurant, she'd been fighting mixed emotions. She first thought he was obnoxious, then gorgeous, and finally just plain frustrating. Sitting on the bed, a towel wrapped around her, she Googled herself.

"I can't say enough wonderful things about the chef at the Key Lime Garden Inn. Riley Cuthbert knows how to turn simple garden food into a memorable gourmet experience. She is amazing."

"The food was amazing. My husband and I made sure to compliment the chef. If you haven't been to the Key Lime Garden Inn, you must go. You won't regret it."

"I wish I could steal Riley Cuthbert away from the Key Lime Garden Inn and hire her as my personal chef."

Pleased that Andrew might have seen these very reviews, her confidence soared.

She finished getting ready and when she entered the kitchen Iris whistled. "Look at you all dressed up."

Riley took a couple of grapes off the counter and popped them into her mouth. "He better get here soon. I'm starving."

Voices from the back porch caught Riley's attention. Whispering, Riley asked, "Which guests are outside?"

"No guests," Iris answered. "It's just Millie and Linda St. James."

"Are you serious? I'll kill her," Riley said.

"Who?"

"Millie. I told her not to say anything to Linda about Andrew. Linda is here because she wants to get a look at him."

"Whatever for?"

Riley rolled her eyes. "I guess Andrew was in some magazine and she thinks he's dreamy."

Iris smiled. "Well, she's right, don't you think?"

Just then, Andrew came through the front door.

"That's him," Riley whispered. "We're out of here before Millie hears his voice."

"Have fun."

Riley ran to the front door and took Andrew's hand. "Let's go."

As she pulled him out the door, he laughed. "This is a strange turn of events. Earlier today you were kicking me out this very door, now you can't wait to be with me. I think I like this."

"Never mind that. I'll explain later."

They got in his car and made it out onto the main road before Millie and Linda could stop them.

Harold's was well-known as one of the best restaurants in Southwest Florida. Riley had planned to eat there eventually, and now she was getting her chance.

"Have you always wanted to own a restaurant?" she asked Andrew.

"Not really. I mean I always loved to cook, but owning a restaurant was never in the cards. Somehow, I was smart enough to understand just how much work it takes to run a restaurant."

Riley nodded. "I know what you mean. My sister and brother-in-law opened a restaurant in Sanibel last year. Not only that, but they also have a new baby so they're exhausted all the time. She lives so close but we never get time to see each other."

"What's the name of their restaurant?"

"Tropical Vegan. I didn't think there were that many people who were vegan, but apparently it's a real thing. Grace and Connor have made a real success of the place."

"I've eaten there," he said.

"You're not vegan, are you?"

"No, not at all but that's the point isn't it? They've made a success of the place because the food is so good people don't miss the animal products. They don't appeal to only vegans. Everyone enjoys their food."

When they ordered dinner, Riley expected Andrew to take over and work to impress her with his knowledge of Harold's food and specific wines, but that didn't happen.

Instead, he let Riley order for herself and only added what he considered his favorite entrees. He didn't talk about himself much, instead asking her questions about her childhood, her family, her job and stayed clear of any past relationships. He was engaging and inquisitive and clearly did everything he could to make Riley feel as if she was the only other person in the room.

She sipped her wine and held back a giggle thinking about Millie's crush on Andrew. He could tell there was something she was hiding and so, she decided to share Millie's obsession with him.

"I'm sorry, I think you should know that you have two

admirers that undoubtedly will still be up and waiting for us to return to the inn tonight."

"Oh? Who might that be?"

She explained about the sexiest man magazine article and the reason she was so quick to drag him to the car earlier. "I'm really sorry to put you through this, but I can't be certain they won't be there. Knowing Millie, she probably still has that magazine and will want an autograph."

Clearly embarrassed, Andrew looked down at the table. "I'm never going to live that down. I had nothing to do with it. The woman who wrote that article never contacted me before putting my picture in the magazine. I was going to make a fuss about it but the truth is that it would have given it more attention than I wanted. In the end, I decided to let it go."

Riley couldn't stop smiling. "I imagine it brought in a few more customers to your restaurant though."

He laughed. "That it did…mostly women of course."

Andrew paid the check and pulled Riley's chair out. "We could always stay out much later to increase our odds of avoiding my two fans."

"I'm afraid you don't know Millie and Linda. They'll still be at the inn even if it's midnight. You might as well face the music and get it over with. It won't matter if they miss you tonight. They'll be back the next time you come around."

Andrew put his hand on her lower back as they walked to the car. Before they got inside, he held her close and looked into her eyes. "Does that mean I get a second date?"

"I think our third encounter went well, don't you?"

"Yes, indeed."

"Well then, I think we can risk a fourth."

Riley was right when she predicted Linda and Millie would be waiting. Sure enough, Millie had the magazine and a pen ready and waiting for Andrew's autograph.

Riley was amused and slightly irritated because with Millie

and Linda hanging on his every word there was no opportunity for a goodnight kiss, and for reasons she couldn't say, that bothered her more than anything else.

Chelsea smiled as she fanned herself, rocking on her front porch. She couldn't stop thinking of the handsome Italian who'd swept her off her feet only a few days earlier. The Captiva sun matched the heat she'd experienced in Italy. Florida was known for being hot in July, but today was worse than usual.

She was about to go inside her air conditioned house when Maggie appeared at the bottom of her front steps with a little dog at the end of a pink leash.

Pointing to the fluff ball, Chelsea asked, "Am I imagining things or is that a dog?"

Maggie and her new pup climbed the stairs. "I wanted you to meet Lexi." She placed Lexi on Chelsea's lap and sat in the rocking chair next to her.

Refusing to touch the dog, Chelsea shook her head.

"I knew you guys were talking about getting a dog, but I had no idea you'd do it right now. You know I'm not a dog person, Maggie."

"How can you not love her? Look at that face. Her owner passed away and she needed a home. We just had to rescue her. Isn't she cute?"

After circling twice, Lexi curled up on Chelsea's lap, her big brown eyes looking up at her.

"Look at that, she already loves you. Lexi, this is your Aunt Chelsea."

Chelsea felt uncomfortable, but looked at Lexi and did her best to be polite. "Hello. Don't pee on anything."

Looking back at Maggie, she pleaded, "Can you take her? I'd like to get some iced tea. Would you like a glass?"

"Sure, thanks."

The cool air hit Chelsea's face when she opened the door. Although ready to move inside, she decided to stay on the porch now that the dog was visiting.

She returned with two glasses and gave Maggie hers. "Isn't it too hot for the dog?"

"It's too hot for any of us to be honest. That's why I thought we'd take our walk early. What are your plans for the day?"

Chelsea resumed her fanning.

"To be honest, I don't have the energy for much more than this. Jacqui Hutchins said she was going to come over around four o'clock to talk about her ideas for the gallery. I told you about this before we all went to Italy."

Maggie nodded. "I remember. Do you think you'll do it?"

"I don't know. I have to think about it. I'm not sure I want to start and open a business. There's a lot to running an art gallery. Plus I'm worried about the difference in our ages. I'm old enough to be Jackie's mother. If we were to go into business together, I worry that we'll be at odds every day. I don't have any children and I'm not going to start having one now."

Maggie laughed. "You see problems where there aren't any. You and Jacqui worked together painting for an entire summer and got along just fine. I'll admit there were moments of friction, but that was because she was dealing with her family issues, and honestly I think you were a stabilizing influence for her. I think Jacqui grew into a mature adult woman during that time and look at her now. She's grown so much. I think you should be flattered that she admires you enough to ask you to open the gallery with her."

Chelsea nodded. "You're right, she's a lovely young woman."

"So? What's really bothering you?"

Chelsea shrugged. "I don't know. I think I'm starting to feel my age."

"Seriously? Who was it that I saw dancing for hours at the wedding? That was you wasn't it?"

"That was the Italian wine and Limoncello talking. I think I might have danced one too many times. Maybe it's time I accept that I'm not a kid anymore."

"This isn't like you to talk this way. You're scaring me," Maggie said.

Suddenly introspective, Chelsea watched as a blue heron flew by, its wings spread wide.

"At what age do you think women lose their passion for life?"

"Is that what they do? I didn't know that. Why would you say a thing like that?"

Chelsea shrugged. "I don't know. It seems there are so many forces in our world sending older women the message that it's time to slow down and walk toward the exit. Everywhere you look the world centers around the young…the beautiful…the healthy…the strong…the rich. If you don't fit that mold, society tells us that our value is reduced. I'm just wondering at what age does that happen…forty?…fifty?"

Maggie sighed. "I don't know. Look at my mother. She's going to be eighty in a few weeks and she shows no sign of slowing down. If she were here right now and you were to ask her, I know what she'd say. She'd say, 'Maggie, my dear, the world needs to catch up with me.'"

They laughed at that, and for a brief moment Chelsea felt hope for the future. "If we could only bottle your mother's spirit, we'd make a fortune."

Maggie got up and kissed Chelsea's cheek. "Speaking of my mother, I've got to go. I'm supposed to have lunch with her today and I still have lots of errands on my list before then."

"Oh please let me go with you? I could spend a few hours around that woman."

"Of course. I'm sure she'd love to see you. I'll come by and pick you up at twelve thirty. I'm supposed to be over there at one o'clock."

"Perfect. I'll be ready."

Maggie looked at Lexi. "Say, goodbye to Aunt Chelsea, Lexi. Tell her we'll see her soon."

Rolling her eyes, Chelsea waved at the pup.

"I can't wait."

CHAPTER 8

*M*aggie's mother, Sarah Garrison, had only recently moved into her new condo at Marina Bluff Estates, and so far as she could tell, her mother seemed pleased with her new surroundings.

"You mean to tell me that your mother hasn't complained once about the place?" Chelsea asked.

Maggie shook her head, "Nope. Not once. I'm starting to worry that she isn't well. It's not like Mom to get along with everyone."

"Well, I guess we'll find out soon enough. I don't see her car in the driveway. Are you sure she remembered you were coming for lunch?"

"I called her this morning to remind her. She accused me of thinking she had dementia."

Chelsea laughed. "Oh good. She's exactly as I remember her."

Maggie knocked on the door and, when her mother didn't answer, rang the bell.

"I hear her voice," Chelsea said as she started for the backyard.

"Mom?" Maggie called out.

"Back here. I'm pruning my roses."

54

"What happened to your car?"

"That old thing? I sold it to Mr. Howard. He's one of the residents here. Didn't you see my golf cart out front? Hello, Chelsea dear. How nice that you're going to join us for lunch."

"Mom, you bought a golf cart?" Maggie asked.

"Yes I did. Why? Did I need to get your permission first?"

Chelsea quietly chuckled, but Maggie wasn't finding the humor in her mother's response.

"Of course not. I'm just surprised. How are you going to get places off the property?"

Sarah shrugged. "Where do I go? Everything I need is on property. I get my hair done here, my bank is here, my grocery shopping is here. I don't need to leave unless I drive over to Captiva and in that case, you can come get me."

"I guess you have a point."

"Let me put my hat away and get my purse. The restaurant isn't far but this place has many more acres than I realized. We'll have lunch over in the Sandbar section Wait till you see the food. You can eat as much as you want for one price. It's incredible."

With only a small appetite, the idea of eating mass quantities of food was unappealing to Maggie. While her mother went inside, Maggie looked at Chelsea and rolled her eyes.

"Can you believe her? I honestly think that she sees getting tons of food at one sitting is somehow pulling one over on the facility. You watch, she'll have plastic bags in her purse ready to take further advantage of the situation."

"Will they let her do that?" Chelsea asked.

"I doubt it. My guess is that we'll be stopped at the door on the way out. Check out her purse. If it's really big, I already know that she's going in for the kill."

Chelsea couldn't stop giggling. "Your mother is one for the books."

"Shhh, here she comes. Look, see what I mean?" she said pointing to her mother's large shoulder bag.

Maggie didn't say a word when they got in the car, instead was an obedient daughter following her mother's directions to the restaurant.

"No, don't take that parking space. It's too close to that awful car. Look at how banged up it is. Trust me, it didn't get that way driving to the supermarket," Sarah instructed.

When Maggie parked too far from the restaurant, her mother insisted they back out and find a spot closer to the front door.

Maggie was already frustrated by the time they slid into the booth. "How often do you come here to eat?"

"Not often. It's a long drive in the golf cart. I usually eat at one of the closer restaurants. The food here is amazing so you'll be happy we came."

They looked over the menu and ordered their food. Sarah looked at her watch. "They move quickly here too. You'll see."

"Are you in a hurry?" Maggie asked.

"No, I've got a few hours before I meet my friends."

"It's nice that you've already made friends," Chelsea said.

"Yes, well, most are women, which is fine...I guess."

"You guess?" Maggie asked.

"Now don't go making a fuss, it's just that it would be nice to meet someone...you know, a companion of sorts."

Maggie understood exactly what her mother was saying, and although she wasn't thrilled about talking to her mother about it, she could understand the need for company from a man."

"You haven't been here more than a few weeks, Mom. Give it time. I'm sure you'll meet someone."

"I'm sure you're right, Maggie, dear. It's just that there are so many more women than men down here. I know you're probably biased, but there are some lovely women and only so many men to go around."

Chelsea almost spit out her iced tea, and Maggie thought it absurd to be advising her mother on how to get a man.

"Look at it this way, Mom. Remember how you used to tell

me what will be, will be? You just have to let things develop naturally. You can't force this. The right partner will show up one of these days when you least expect it."

Sarah took a sip of her wine spritzer and rolled her eyes. "He better show up soon, I'm not getting any younger you know."

———

Maggie walked in on Paolo cleaning the floor with the pet spray they'd bought at the local hardware store. Lexi stood nearby looking like she'd done something wrong but wasn't exactly sure what.

"That's the second time today. Maybe we need to hire a trainer to teach Lexi to go outside," she said.

"She's just nervous, that's all. She's in a new place with strangers. She's old enough to know to go outside. I think this is temporary," Paolo explained.

Maggie smiled at the way Paolo seemed to forgive Lexi for anything she might do wrong. The two had bonded and Maggie loved seeing Paolo and Lexi become best friends so quickly.

"We've got mail from the Town Hall," Maggie said as she opened the envelope. "Oh no! This can't be right," she lamented.

"What? What is it?"

"The town wants us to stop the construction on the cottage and cabana. This is a cease and desist letter. We have to stop immediately."

"Let me see that."

Paolo read the letter and his face turned red with anger. "They can't do this. We applied for and were granted a building permit. They're saying that we misrepresented the project and that the town did not authorize the building of a cabana next to the cottage. They say they only approved the cottage but now we must stop that because of this violation. This is outrageous. It's only a cabana for heaven's sake."

"Did we not mention the cabana when we filed for the permit?"

Paolo shook his head, "No, I don't think we decided on the cabana until after we got the permit. Come on, Maggie. It's a cabana. It's not like it's another building. They're making a big deal out of nothing. I'm going up there."

"Wait. You need to calm down first. I'm not having you go up there the way you are right now."

"I'm fine. I'll take a few deep breaths and then I'll walk up calmly to the Town Hall and calmly ask how we can resolve this."

"You're not going alone. Lexi can stay in her crate. You and I will go together."

"Fine. Someone is going to have to explain what is going on. There's no reason to stop construction, and I'm going to make sure they hear what I have to say."

Paolo was already halfway down the stairs when Maggie put Lexi in her crate and grabbed her purse. She said a silent prayer.

Please don't let Paolo make things worse.

The Town Hall was rarely buzzing with activity, and when they went to the clerk's window, no one was there.

"Hello?" Paolo called out.

"Where is everyone? It's like a ghost town here."

They walked up and down the hall, and eventually saw a woman at the Treasurer's desk.

"Can I help you?" she asked.

"Hey, Marsha," Maggie said.

"Maggie. How have you been? I haven't seen you since the Christmas Parade. You know everyone is still talking about how wonderful your children's double wedding was."

Maggie could tell that Paolo was getting impatient.

"Thank you, Marsha. Listen, is there someone we can talk to

about a building permit? We're in the middle of construction and received this letter."

Paolo handed the letter to the woman.

"Oh my goodness. I know nothing about this. Let me look in my computer to see if there are any other notes."

Paolo began to pace while Maggie kept things cordial.

"Nope. There's nothing more than what you have in this letter."

"Let me talk to Roger Harrison. He's the one who signed this letter," Paolo insisted.

"Unfortunately, Roger left for vacation yesterday. He's on a cruise to Iceland."

Marsha looked at Maggie. "Doesn't that sound heavenly? I'd love to see Iceland. Did you know that the people there believe in fairies? I'm serious. No joke, they really do. At least fifty-percent of them do. They call them 'hidden people'. Isn't that something?"

Maggie thought the information fascinating; however, her immediate concern was keeping Paolo from climbing the wall.

"Maybe another time we can talk about this, Marsha. In the meantime, what do you think we should do about this? As we mentioned, the construction is already underway and…"

"I'm sorry, Maggie, but I think you're going to have to wait until Roger gets back."

"And when will that be?" Paolo asked.

"Not for another two weeks. I think it's a twelve-day cruise. I'm really sorry, but Roger has final say on this."

"Who is Roger's boss? Maybe I need to talk to him."

By this time, Marsha looked like she was ready to either call the police or punch Paolo in the nose.

"Roger is the Building Inspector and his boss is Michael Saccone. He's the Building Official who oversees everything but you can't talk to him today because he's on a construction project meeting off-island."

"When will Mr. Saccone be in the office?"

"Tomorrow. Would you like to leave a message?"

"Yes, you can tell Mr. Saccone that I need to talk to him about this as soon as possible."

"I'll tell him," Marsha said. Passing a piece of paper in front of Paolo, she added, "Leave your telephone number and I'll have him call you as soon as he can."

Paolo left more than his cellphone number. He also added that as owner of the Key Lime Garden Inn he expected the Building Official to move quickly to resolve his problem. He was about to include a few threatening words when Maggie put her hand on his arm.

"Honey, I think you've said enough."

Paolo put the pen down and stormed toward the front door.

"I'm sorry, Marsha. You can understand how upsetting this is."

"Of course. I'm sure Mr. Saccone will resolve the problem as soon as he gets back."

Maggie caught up with Paolo, who wasn't happy with her apology to Marsha.

"You didn't have to apologize for me, Maggie. I'm not the one who is wrong here."

Maggie wanted to say more but decided to let it go since Paolo's mood was getting worse by the minute. She could only hope that little Lexi might help ease the tension and turn her husband back into the sweet and gentle man that everyone loved. If not, the next twenty-four hours were going to be miserable for anyone who crossed his path.

When they got home, Paolo walked to the construction site with Lexi running behind him all the way. Maggie watched as he picked Lexi up in his arms and cuddled her close to his face. Smiling, she turned back to the inn and left the two of them alone.

By dinnertime, it appeared that Lexi had worked her magic. Paolo was his usual charming self, and Maggie enjoyed a peaceful evening otherwise known as the calm before the storm.

CHAPTER 9

*J*acqui Hutchins left her parents' house and drove to Chelsea Marsden's place on Captiva Island. Ever since she lived with Chelsea two summers ago, Jacqui thought of the island as her home away from home and gave considerable thought to moving there permanently.

She didn't like admitting that she'd come to depend on her father's money to support herself, but she was convinced that soon, she'd be able to make all the money she needed to live comfortably.

Graduate studies over, Jacqui focused her energy on the future and the possibility of opening an art gallery on the island of Captiva. There were plenty of galleries on Sanibel, but not any on Captiva and that seemed like an opportunity. She couldn't do it alone, however. She needed Chelsea's talent and realistic perspective on running a business.

Jacqui was used to getting her way and since money was no object, there were hardly any barriers to reaching her goal. The bigger problem was Chelsea herself. Chelsea was no pushover and Jacqui had serious doubts that the woman would help her fulfill her dreams. They'd worked well together but most importantly, Chelsea was an expressive and visionary artist and one with whom Jacqui felt a kinship.

Reciting the same mantra during the drive to Captiva, Jacqui pulled into Chelsea's driveway.

Come on, Chelsea. Please say yes. Please say yes.

The front door was unlocked and so Jacqui called out as she went inside.

"Chelsea?" Jacqui called.

"Out here on the lanai," Chelsea answered.

"I should have known you'd be out here painting. Whatever you're working on, it looks amazing."

Jacqui looked down at Chelsea's paint and back up at the canvas. "No watercolor?"

Chelsea shook her head. "Nope. I'm using acrylics today. Come on in and sit. Would you like something to drink?"

"No, thanks. I'm good."

"How's your father doing? I hear he wants to get back to work. Isn't that a bit too soon after the stroke."

Jacqui laughed. "Tell that to him. I'm surprised we've been able to keep him at home this long. He's stubborn and opinionated and won't take no for an answer."

Chelsea smiled. "Sounds like someone I know."

Jacqui got the inference. "Does that mean you'll say yes to my idea?"

Chelsea put her brush down. "Let's just say I'm considering it."

"Considering is good. What do you need to know from me to help you decide?"

Chelsea faced Jacqui. "For one, whose work are you planning to show for the Grand Opening? Surely not mine."

"No. Not yours. I have several connections already in New York. I think I can get one artist in particular who is an incredible talent. I adore her work."

"What's her name?"

"Marguerite Verne. She's been living in this country for the last three years but she was born in Paris. I've already contacted her and told her what I was planning. She was tickled pink when I said that we'd like to display her work in our new gallery...as soon as it's opened, that is."

"Isn't that a bit like putting the cart before the horse?"

"Chelsea, listen to me. We can do this. I've found a fantastic piece of commercial real estate. It's down the end of Laika Lane. It's perfect. You have to come check it out."

"Laika Lane? I don't know of any commercial property there...only houses."

"Well, it is a house that's been zoned for business because there was a tackle and bait store right there once before. It's abandoned now and only a stone's throw walk from the stores. There's lots of parking and...well, you have to have a good imagination to see it as a gallery. But, we can make it work."

"I don't want to buy another property on Captiva, Jacqui."

"I'll buy it. I have the money."

Chelsea raised an eyebrow. "You mean your father has the money. Jacqui, I don't want to sound ungrateful. I love that I was the first person you thought of when you decided to own a gallery, but this is too much of a start-up...literally. I'm familiar with the property you're talking about. It's abandoned for a reason. I think I'll have to pass on this one."

"The gallery or the property? I only ask because we can fix one problem. It doesn't have to be that property. We can keep looking. Please, Chelsea. Don't throw the idea of opening a gallery away. Sit on it some more. I'll see where else we could open it. Say you'll keep thinking about it."

Jacqui could see that she was getting to Chelsea. "I hate to burst your bubble, but the idea seems fraught with obstacles I'm just not ready for at this point in my life. I'll tell you what. Why don't *you* open a gallery and I'll put up several of my pieces to get you started? You've got the financial backing so you don't need my money. What you need is confidence to get out there on your own and make something of yourself. Don't fall back into the little Jacqui that I knew a few years ago. You've grown into a strong and independent woman. Your talent is enough to make the gallery a success."

Jacqui had never considered doing anything on her own. She thought about Chelsea's words and could only agree with her. "Really? You think I can do this?"

Chelsea reached out to her. "I know you can. You've got what it takes. You're not afraid of taking chances. At least not the Jacqui I know. Besides, you're not alone. You've not only got your family's support, but you also have mine. I'll be here every step of the way. Maggie, Sarah and Trevor too. We all will do whatever it takes to help you make a success of this."

For the first time in her life, Jacqui felt a glimmer of hope that she could get out from under the Hutchins name. Every member of her family was a financial success. She worried that she'd never be able to measure up to what they'd accomplished.

She finally understood that her idea of success looked nothing like what her family members had achieved. Nor did she want it to. She was her own person, and a talented artist. With Chelsea's help, she knew that talent was her ticket to the future she'd wanted all her life.

"Thanks, Chelsea. I appreciate your faith in me. I guess it's time I start having faith in myself."

"Sounds right to me," Chelsea answered. "How'd you like to put on an apron and hoist a canvas up on that frame? Nothing like painting in the middle of the afternoon to get your spirits excited."

"I'd love it...and thank you Chelsea. I mean it. You always know exactly what I need to hear."

"No problem, kiddo. Let's see what they taught you at that fancy New York school."

Beth never felt more broken than she did sitting at her desk at work. For all her thinking about quitting, she still hadn't said a word to anyone but her husband. Her anxiety growing in the pit of her stomach, she sipped her coffee and hoped the warm liquid would soothe her.

After several minutes of ruminating over her situation, panic set in and she felt as if she was suffocating. Needing fresh air and the sun on her face, she grabbed her coffee and ran out of the building to the park across the street.

She took several deep breaths to calm herself and within a few minutes felt better. Months earlier she had sat on this very bench pulling her winter coat close and sipping a cup of hot chocolate. She'd just been married and felt like she had the whole world in front of her.

Now, only seven months later, she felt lost and angry that she'd spent so many years working toward a career that now felt so completely wrong for her.

She thought about her deceased father and how her first thoughts of law school were dominated by her desire to please him. Daniel Wheeler measured a person's value by their accomplishments and that knowledge now stung Beth to her core.

It was love she'd wanted from him, not approval, and she wasn't the only one afflicted with this struggle. Her sister, Sarah, too, made most of her decisions based on their father's reaction.

Sarah's ambition never matched their father's but that didn't stop her from climbing the financial corporate ladder, nonetheless. In time, Sarah learned the lesson that Beth was now realizing.

Their father was gone and Beth would have to find a way to live her life on her terms and no one else's. If that meant throwing away years going down the wrong road, she'd have to right herself and steer the course of her life in a new direction. The only problem was that Beth had no idea what that direction was.

Sipping her coffee, she watched as three women guided two rows of children, no more than four years old, through the park. A rope kept them connected and safe as they crossed the street. Beth couldn't help but smile at how cute they all looked. Having children was definitely in her future, but for now, she wanted her first married year to be only her and Gabriel.

An elderly man sat alone on another bench. He threw bread crumbs to the pigeons and soon was mobbed by a throng of birds.

A young couple sitting further down had headphones on and were glued to watching the screen on their cellphones. Beth smiled, thinking they were probably texting one another. She wanted to rip their headphones off and insist they turn to one another and communicate eye-to-eye.

She looked up at the building and sighed. Sitting outside all day wasn't going to solve anything. She knew that she couldn't hide any longer. It was time to tell her boss, Mitchell, that she was quitting and be done with it once and for all.

Don't quit until you have something else, Beth. You still need the money after all. Don't be stupid.

"Mitchell's been looking for you for the last hour. Where've you been?" her assistant asked.

Beth didn't answer, instead going directly to Mitchell's office.

"Hey, Meredith said you wanted to see me?"

"Yeah, I've got something I want you to check out. We've got another child murder on our hands. I'm pretty sure we're looking at a molester on this one. I'd like you to…"

"No," Beth answered, interrupting him.

Mitchell stared at her. "I'm sorry? Did you say no?"

"That's right, Mitchell. I can't do it again. I just can't."

It was more than shocking to her when instead of being angry, his voice softened. "Let's sit down for a minute. Tell me what's going on? Is everything all right with you and Gabriel?"

"Oh, Mitchell…come on. You know better than to ask me

that. Everything is fine at home. It's not about my personal life. This is about this job and what it's doing to me. When I decided to become a prosecuting attorney, I felt so empowered...so ready to take on the world and fight the bad guys."

"And, you're good at it," he said.

"I'm good at it because I have a passion for helping people who can't help themselves. But these days I'm realizing that it's not a passion at all...more accurately I'm just an empath... someone who needs to nurture and care about others. That doesn't mean I need to go after the worst in our society. I don't think I realized just how many evil people there are in the world."

"Whoa...wait a minute. I think that's a huge jump to make because you're struggling with the job. Yeah, there are bad people but there are many who are good, kind and caring. Maybe what you need is a leave of absence to think about this."

Beth shook her head. "I've done that already...remember? No, I have to face facts. This isn't the career for me. I don't know what I'm going to do, but at least I do know that."

Mitchell nodded. "How about you take two weeks anyway? I don't want you walking out the door today with the thought that you won't come back. Take your vacation. Go away and relax and really give this more thought. I don't want you to regret your decision...whatever it may be."

"I don't need to take two weeks to decide. If I do that, just like before, I might come back when I shouldn't. No, I've made up my mind. I've got to quit."

Mitchell ran his hand through his hair and sighed. "Okay, listen, this is what we'll do. Take three weeks paid vacation. You still work here and that's that. If, in three weeks, you still feel the same, I'll accept your resignation, but not one minute before."

Beth smiled. "Who knew you were such a nice guy?"

He laughed. "Don't let that get around. I've got a reputation to uphold."

CHAPTER 10

*L*auren let days go by before approaching her husband once again about her ideas for their children's education. Convinced they needed to move before the summer was over, she couldn't put it off any longer.

"How was work?" he asked as she dropped her bag onto the living room sofa and joined him in the kitchen.

"Busy as usual. Something smells good. What are we having?"

"Chicken piccata…your favorite."

"Oh, yum. What's the occasion?"

Jeff laughed. "The occasion is that chicken breasts were on sale."

"Oh, I see. It's awfully quiet. Where are the girls?"

Jeff put out two wine glasses on the kitchen island and filled them with Pinot Grigio.

"The girls are over at the Parquets' for a sleepover. I thought it best they stay there while you and I talk about whatever is going on in that head of yours."

Lauren took a sip of her wine and then looked at him. "I guess we've been married long enough that you can tell when I want to have a serious discussion."

He smiled. "That and the fact that you called and said you'd be home early. You don't come home early unless you've got something on your mind. Dare I ask? Does this have anything to do with you wanting the girls to be homeschooled?"

Lauren wanted her chance to explain her feelings and for Jeff to take her concerns seriously.

"Can we sit in the living room and really talk about this?" she asked.

"Lead on," he answered, taking his wine glass with him.

"What I'd like you to consider is the possibility of taking a year or two and giving homeschooling a real chance. But...I want to do more than just homeschool. I want to expose the girls to a different education, one that they can't get from a classroom. I want the four of us...I mean, five of us soon, to travel to another country. I want the girls to learn a different culture and to speak another language."

Jeff looked shocked at her explanation. "Lauren, this is a complete change from the way we've lived our lives thus far. I understand your desire to teach them more than they're getting in school, but can't we do that living in Massachusetts?"

"Of course we can. But, I don't think they'll get the most out of the experience. Unless they're living and learning among the people they're studying, I'm not sure the impact would be the same. I want them to truly know what it's like to live in another culture...to see how others live."

Stunned, it seemed to Lauren that her husband was running out of ways to oppose the idea.

"I'm at a loss for words. I mean, I don't know anyone else who has done this. Don't you think it might be a good idea to talk to people who've taken this journey?"

Lauren's face lit up. "I'm so glad you said that. I agree, so I've looked into it and as it happens, the Trainors at our church did it for two years. As a matter of fact, they have a presentation along with a video they're showing next Thursday night. I think we should go and talk to them. Maybe even bring the girls because I know their children will be there."

Jeff hesitated. "I don't know...This feels so crazy...I..."

"Please, Jeff. Let's just go listen to what they have to say before you say no. At least we can hear the pros and cons about it. I mean, I love the idea but there is a lot I don't know either. If it really seems too far-fetched then we'll find another way to expose the girls to different cultures, and I'll drop the whole thing. Although, I still think we should seriously consider home-schooling."

"What about your work? Your business? You've gone through so much in these last few months. You've struggled to get the place back up and running, and now you'll throw all that away?"

"I can always go back to real estate, the girls are growing and I won't be able to get these years back. I've talked to Nell and Brian about possibly keeping the place going while we're gone and maybe even buying the business. I'm not saying I'm ready to sell, but I did want them to think about it if the situation arises."

Lauren could see an acceptance on Jeff's face. It was hard to dispute getting more information than it was to forget the whole thing.

"Okay. Just remember that I'm only agreeing to hearing what they have to say...nothing more."

Lauren clinked her wine glass against Jeff's. "That's all I'm asking. Thank you, honey. Thank you so much."

Maggie didn't want to upset Paolo, but Marsha Worthington's phone call was bad news.

"I'm so sorry, Maggie, but Mr. Saccone won't be in today after all. I didn't have the heart to tell him about Paolo."

"For heaven's sake, why not?" Maggie asked.

"I'm not supposed to tell anyone but his sister is very sick and in the hospital. He's been back and forth there for weeks and I think she's in Hospice now."

"Oh, my goodness, I'm so sorry," Maggie responded. "I'll let Paolo know. Please let us know when he is able to talk with us and thank you for giving us this news. We'll keep it to ourselves."

"Thank you, Maggie. I'll stay in touch."

Maggie ended the call and looked out the window toward the back of the property. Paolo was puttering around the construction site with Lexi keeping pace with his every move. The thought of telling Paolo this latest news made her already nasty headache all the more painful. Nonetheless, the bad news would have to be delivered.

She put a hat on and walked through the garden to the framed cottage. "I just got off the phone with Marsha from the Town Hall. I'm sorry to say that you won't be able to talk to Michael Saccone anytime soon."

"What? Why not?"

"He's at the hospital. His sister is dying and I guess it's not common knowledge. Marsha wasn't supposed to tell me this so we better keep this information private."

Paolo sat on the bench next to the koi pond and Lexi jumped onto his lap.

"Honey, I know this is frustrating, but think of it this way. It's just a delay. Somehow there was a mix-up and it will get resolved in time."

"Yes, but how much time?"

She joined him on the bench. "Well, it's not like we live in a big city where we'd have to deal with lots of red tape. This is an island where everyone knows everyone. It's just a delay."

Resigned to the situation, Paolo nodded. "I guess we don't have much choice."

"Wait. Wasn't Saccone Byron Jameson's wife's maiden name?"

"I have no idea. How do you remember these things?" he asked.

"I'm pretty sure. Chelsea will know. Is it possible that Byron Jameson's wife is dying and he doesn't want anyone to know?"

"Why wouldn't he want people to know? It's not like she's done something wrong. The poor woman is dying."

"Yes, but you don't know Byron like I do. He hates for anyone to know his business. He's very private."

Paolo doubted Maggie's opinion. "Are you telling me that Captiva Island's Christmas Santa is a private person? The guy who spends most of his time at the Bubble Room bar? Somehow, private is not how I think of Byron."

"I'm going to get to the bottom of this. Something doesn't feel right. I'll go over to Chelsea's to see if she knows anything. I'll be back in a jiff."

Sweat dripping from her face, Chelsea answered the door.

"What in the world? Are you all right?"

"I'm fine. I just finished my Zumba class online. I thought you said you were going to join me one of these days."

"I was going to, but to look at your face, I think I need to reconsider."

"My face might look bad but my heart is getting healthy so there's that. So, what's going on?"

"Do you know anything about Byron's wife?"

"Louise? Not much. Why?"

"Do you know what her maiden name was? I have a hunch about something but I thought I'd check with you. Is it Saccone by any chance?"

"I think you're right but I can't be sure. I do remember that it was an Italian name," Chelsea said. "Your best bet is to ask Linda St. James. You know how she's the island's busybody. I bet she'll not only know her last name but her parents' names, how many siblings she has and what she wore on her first date with Byron."

Maggie laughed. "That sounds like Linda for sure. My only issue with asking Linda is that the minute I leave her place she'll be passing the word around the island that I was questioning her about Louise."

"Good point. Maybe there is a way to look online. I use Ancestry all the time for things like this. Let me get my computer and we'll see what we can find."

"Thanks, Chelsea. I knew if anyone would know how to snoop to find out, it would be you."

Maggie was excited to see what the Ancestry website could do. "This is amazing."

"I love it," Chelsea said. "I did my DNA test too and found lots of relatives all over the country. The best part is looking at this map to see where my ancestors come from."

"Cool. So, how do we find out about Louise?"

"We just do a search on her name as it is now. Plus, I'll put Byron's name in too as her husband."

Chelsea filled in the form and hit search. "See all these possible names on the right?"

"Are all those Louise?" Maggie asked.

"No. One of these will be her, we just have to search for ones that make sense based on her age and geography."

They scrolled down searching for the right Louise Jameson. "There she is. Look, it also says Louise Saccone. That's got to be her."

Chelsea nodded. "Looks like it. Now, do you want to tell me why we did this? What's going on?"

Maggie explained the problem with the building permit and wondered if Byron had anything to do with the cease and desist letter.

"Why would Byron not want you to build the cabana? It doesn't make any sense," Chelsea asked.

Maggie shook her head. "I have no idea, but somehow, I'm going to find out exactly what's going on."

CHAPTER 11

*W*hen news came that her best friend Emma and her new husband, Gareth, were coming to Florida, Sarah's excitement was palpable. Although she loved spending time with her children, she needed a break from the Paw Patrol television show.

She knew the theme song by heart and found herself singing it while doing the dishes.

"My brain has gone to mush," she said aloud to no one in particular.

"What did you say?" Trevor asked, handing her his tie.

"Oh, nothing. Just talking to myself...yet again."

She deftly fastened his tie and planted a kiss on his lips and one on his cheek.

"You look mighty handsome, Mr. Hutchins. Tell me, are there going to be any beautiful women at your meeting today? I'm only asking because I'll leave the lipstick stain on your face for all to see."

Trevor grabbed a piece of paper towel and looked at his reflection in the microwave. Rubbing his face he smiled. "Nope, only ugly people at my meetings. I insist on it," he teased.

"Did I tell you that Mom is coming over to watch the kids while I get my nails done? I didn't want to bother her but Debbie was busy and I really needed the afternoon to myself."

"That's great, hon. What time are we meeting Emma and Gareth?"

"We need to be at Doc Ford's at seven, and I need you to be on your best behavior."

"When am I not?"

"Well, I remember you telling me that you weren't that fond of Gareth. I don't want Emma to feel like her best friend's husband disapproves of her marriage."

"Sarah, that was when they first met. I didn't know the man. If Emma is happy then I'm happy. I'm sure he's a nice guy. It took a lot for her to get married. I can't imagine she'd marry a jerk."

"Good. I'm glad to hear it. Anyway, you better get going. I heard on the news that traffic to the bridge is slow."

"What else is new?" he said.

Trevor took his briefcase and headed for the door. "Hey, did you forget something?" she asked as she tilted her head to one side, waiting for her kiss.

He dropped the briefcase, leaned down and pulled her into him. Kissing her deeply, they stayed in that embrace for a long time.

"Whoa, what's this? A passionate kiss in the morning usually means someone is feeling guilty about something."

He looked into her eyes and nodded. "I do feel guilty...guilty that I'm leaving the most beautiful wife to go sit in a stuffy conference room listening to the same boring presentation. I miss the old days when I wore jeans, kept my hair long and generally told time by where the sun was in the sky."

Sarah didn't want to say anything to depress Trevor, but she missed those days as well. He looked uncomfortable in a suit and tie, but there was little to be done about it. Today's meeting was about taking the company public and only the proper attire would do.

"Good luck today, honey. I hope things go the way you want."

Trevor picked up his briefcase and blew her a kiss on his way out the door.

"You're coming with me," Maggie insisted.

"What? Why me? Linda and I aren't the best of friends. She probably won't share anything with me around," Chelsea added.

Maggie was certain there was a connection to their construction woes and Byron Jameson's wife, but she couldn't be certain without talking to Linda St. James.

The only problem was Linda herself. The biggest gossip on Captiva Island was not to be messed with. Getting information out of her without Linda suspecting anything could be done, albeit with a carefully planned approach.

Remembering that Linda always stopped at RC Otters for breakfast every morning, Maggie decided to accidently, on purpose, run into Linda there.

"How weird will it look for —the owner of a bed & breakfast —to go to RC Otters for breakfast? It would make much more sense if you and I were going there together. So, hurry up and get in the shower. She's always there between ten and eleven and I don't want to miss my window of opportunity."

"Okay. Okay, I'm going," Chelsea said, mumbling something about a ride or die friend under her breath.

Maggie paced Chelsea's lanai thinking about how best to begin the conversation with Linda. It wouldn't do for them to say hello and move to another table. Maggie needed to invite herself to join Linda for breakfast...not usual, but not unheard of.

Ten minutes had passed and Maggie was getting anxious.

"Are you almost ready?"

"Stop rushing me. Trust me, Linda never leaves her house without her face covered in makeup and not a hair out of place. If I show up like I just got out of bed, she'll not only be suspicious but downright rude. She'd make a comment, I just know it."

Maggie rolled her eyes. "Whatever. You look fine. Let's go."

RC Otters was about one hundred yards from Chelsea's house. They strolled to the restaurant as casually as they could, stopping to say hello to people they knew along the way.

"Maggie Moretti, what in the world are you doing here for breakfast? Did you run out of scones at your place?" Linda said, teasing.

Maggie and Chelsea laughed. "No, not at all. We just thought it would be nice to get out and have breakfast someplace else for a change."

Inviting themselves to join Linda's table was awkward at best given that she was sitting at a single table, but Maggie wasn't deterred.

"What do you say we get a bigger table so Chelsea and I can join you? Would you mind?"

"For heaven's sake, of course not."

The waitress helped set up another table and Linda carried her coffee to join Maggie and Chelsea.

"Well, isn't this nice? Hello, Chelsea, you look well."

"Thank you, Linda," Chelsea answered.

"I don't think the three of us have eaten together since Christmas at the double wedding. Thank you and Paolo again for inviting me. It meant a lot, especially when you realize that not everyone could get an invite," Linda said.

"Yes, well, the property could hold only so many people. I think we did all right, don't you?" Maggie asked her.

The waitress brought more coffee for all three and took their orders.

"Of course, I was happy, but...well, I'm sure you already know there were a few people whose noses were out of joint. I let them know in no uncertain terms exactly what you just said. There was only so much room."

Confused, Maggie asked, "I'm sorry? Someone complained to you about not getting an invitation?"

"Oh, Maggie, please forget I said anything," Linda whispered. "You know how petty people on this island can be."

It suddenly dawned on Maggie that there was one couple in particular that she didn't invite. "Is it possible that one of the people who complained was Byron Jameson?"

Linda's face was a mix of satisfaction and alarm. While it was clear that she wanted Maggie to know of her error in judgment, she didn't want Byron to know that it was she who spilled the beans.

Waiting for an answer, Maggie stared at Linda.

"All I know is he had a few too many at the Bubble Room and started mouthing off to everyone at the bar. I wasn't there of course as I don't drink, however, Nancy and Evelyn were and they mentioned it to me in passing."

In passing? Maggie thought. More like they made a bee-line right to your door as soon as they left the Bubble Room.

"I told them they shouldn't pass this information around town. You know how things get taken out of context. The next thing you know, people aren't speaking to one another."

Their food arrived and Chelsea dug into her pancakes with gusto. Maggie, on the other hand, had lost her appetite but needed to act as if she wasn't upset, so she took a few bites of her scrambled eggs.

Leaning in, Linda whispered further, "You must have heard about his wife, Louise. Poor thing. She doesn't have much time, you know."

Not even this news was enough for Chelsea to pretend to be shocked or at least concerned. Finally, Maggie kicked her under the table and Chelsea sat up straight and swallowed.

"That's terrible," Chelsea said."

"I'm sorry to hear that," Maggie added.

Changing the subject, Linda tried to get information out of Maggie about Andrew Hansen.

"It looks like your chef has made a real catch dating Andrew Hansen. Isn't he gorgeous? I've heard only wonderful things about him. How long have they been dating? Do you think it's serious? Can you imagine if Riley Cuthbert and Andrew Hansen got married? It would be the talk of the island. This is all so exciting, don't you think?"

While Linda babbled on about Andrew and Riley, Maggie ate her breakfast, nodded now and then, and plotted how she'd get to Byron Jameson to patch things up before Louise passed away. She'd need to move quickly and by the looks of things, she'd be better off doing it without Chelsea.

"There's no doubt about it now," Maggie said to Chelsea as they walked back to Chelsea's house. "Somehow, Byron had a hand in influencing Michael Saccone to put a hold on the building permit."

"Don't you think that's a convoluted stretch? I mean, yeah, Byron being mad at you is a thing, but I doubt he's upset enough to punish you and Paolo by rejecting the permit. Besides, I don't think his brother-in-law would allow such intrusion into his job."

Maggie didn't know what to think. "I don't know, Chelsea. I hear what you're saying but stopping the construction because of a silly little cabana is over the top if you ask me."

"It's not a silly little cabana, Maggie. It's a permanent structure and you guys were wrong not to include it when you applied for the permit. You have to look at the big picture here and not adopt conspiracy theories...at least not until you talk to Byron."

"I'm not looking forward to that. Honestly, with what Louise is going through, there really isn't a good time to talk to Byron about this. As a matter of fact I feel awful for making such a big deal about it. I have no problem admitting our mistake, reapplying for the new permit and waiting until it gets approved, but…"

"But…Paolo. Why is he being so stubborn about this?"

Maggie shook her head. "I honestly don't know. Ever since Ciara's wedding he's been moody and difficult to talk to. I'm just glad we got Lexi. She seems to be the only one who can calm him down."

Chelsea laughed. "If Byron had anything to do with this, you'd better keep Lexi close. You might need her to keep Paolo out of jail."

CHAPTER 12

$\mathcal{T}$he low lights and candle centerpieces gave Sweet Melissa's restaurant a romantic feel. Although romance was not the evening's intention, Sarah saw the quiet and calm ambiance of the room as a perfect spot to meet Emma and her new husband Gareth for dinner.

The two couples arrived at the same time, and the host brought them to their table.

"I've been here several times. The food is wonderful," Sarah said.

The waiter handed them menus and filled their glasses with water.

"Can I get anyone something to drink?" he asked.

"I'd like a sangria," Emma answered.

"I'll have the same," Sarah added.

The men ordered their cocktails and the waiter left them to talk.

"How long have you guys been back in Florida?"

"We got here the day before yesterday," Emma answered.

"Emma wanted to go directly to her parents' place, so we've been staying in Naples with them," Gareth added.

"How did that go? Don't tell me. I'm guessing they were less than happy with the fact that you got married and didn't tell them until it was over," Sarah said.

Emma nodded. "Let's just say we had a heated discussion about it, followed by my mother insisting that they throw a party for us so that all their friends could celebrate."

"Will there be enough time? How long are you staying in Florida?" Trevor asked.

"I don't have to be back in New York until the end of the month and Emma took a few weeks off in anticipation of her mother's reaction."

"Dad has been great about the whole thing. It's really my mother who thinks the world is ending because she can't throw a huge wedding. You know me, Sarah. Even if I lived here I'd still probably elope. I'm not the big, fancy wedding type."

Sarah laughed. "Well, at least she still has Jillian. I hear she and Finn are getting serious. At least they looked serious in Italy."

"Yeah, I'm sorry I missed her but I'm making up for it by spending extra time in Florida. As far as how serious she and Finn are, I have no idea. She doesn't tell me anything."

"So Gareth, I understand that you've been working on a new book. When do you think it will be published?"

"Thanks for asking, Trevor, but to be honest, I have no idea. If my editor has any say...never. At least that's how I feel about her constant demands for changes. I was hoping to have it out by the end of the summer, but now...I don't know...more likely Christmas."

Sarah could see how in love the two of them were. Emma took her husband's hand and looked at Sarah. "Gareth can't work on the book too much this summer anyway. He's agreed to do Il Camino di Santiago with me."

"You mean the hike you did before with..."

Sarah felt uncomfortable mentioning Emma's previous boyfriend in front of her new husband.

"With Timothy, yes, and I did it one more time after that. It's such a transformative experience but it's also an individual pilgrimage. I've described my journey to Gareth, but it's no substitute for doing the walk."

"That's fantastic," Sarah said. "Trevor, you remember me telling you when Emma did that before?"

Trevor nodded. "Oh right. That was a long hike to some church in Spain. How many miles are you going to walk?"

"We'll start in Madrid. It's a little over three-hundred kilometers. We're scheduled to do the walk in August. I've taken the whole month off. I can't wait."

Looking at Gareth, Trevor asked, "Are you a religious man?"

It was obvious to Sarah that the question took Gareth by surprise.

"Not at all. If anything, I'd say I'm more of an agnostic than a firm believer."

"But, you're not an atheist?"

"Trevor..." Sarah said, feeling the question confrontational. "I thought the rule is no talk of politics or religion at the dinner table?"

Gareth looked at Sarah and shook his head. "No, it's fine. The truth is that although I was raised a Catholic, I haven't been to church in years. Not because it was inconvenient, but rather because I'm uncertain about the existence of a God."

Shocked by his admission, Sarah wished they'd never started the conversation. Just then, the waiter brought them their drinks and Sarah was grateful for the interruption.

Unyielding, Gareth continued. "I've had personal struggles that have made me question everything, Trevor. Emma has been a light in my life. She's got me feeling hope for the first time in a very long time. However, I'm still on the fence about my faith."

Sarah smiled, remembering her conversation with Emma about the death of Gareth's brother in a car accident.

Emma tried to explain. "You see, Trevor. The pilgrimage is

considered a spiritual walk, but make no mistake, the history is a religious one and continues to be. It's believed that St. James, one of Christ's followers, is buried there. People do the Camino for lots of reasons. Gareth and I have talked about his crisis of faith. I believe he'll find what he's searching for on this walk. I know that I did."

Sarah was moved by Gareth's desire to seek answers regarding his faith.

"You and Trevor should do the walk," Emma said.

Sarah looked at Trevor and smiled. "That will have to remain a dream for now. We've just got back from Italy. I don't see us going overseas anytime soon...not with our three kids anyway."

Trevor looked over at the waiter and whispered, "I think we all should order. The waiter keeps looking at our table. I think he's getting anxious that we're only here for drinks."

Everyone laughed and picked up their menus, but Sarah couldn't stop thinking about Paw Patrol, diapers and after-school soccer games.

The Camino would have to wait...at least for the foreseeable future.

Beth directed the remote control at the tv screen and changed the channel. Between her pink fuzzy slippers, she could see a Hallmark Channel movie. A bag of potato chips and a soda on the coffee table, she wondered whether these were enough to keep her satiated.

Looking at the clock, she had just enough time to watch a movie before placing a take-out order for dinner. She'd already ordered pizza the night before, and figured Gabriel wouldn't go for it a second night in a row.

She'd worry about that when it was time. For now, she pulled a blanket over her and their dog Charlie who was adapting nicely to Beth's new routine.

A knock on the front door startled her. She lifted her body and peered over the top of the sofa.

"Chris! What are you doing here?"

Her brother hadn't called before showing up and that worried her. Christopher always called before driving up to see her. The fact that he hadn't meant something was wrong.

She sat up and pulled the blanket off Charlie, giving Chris a place to sit.

"I thought I'd come to visit my sister. Do I need a better reason than that?" he answered.

She smirked and shook her head. "Who do you think you're talking to? I might be a Walker, but I was born a Wheeler and us Wheelers are always in each other's business. So…spill. Why are you here exactly?"

Christopher went into the kitchen and opened the refrigerator.

"Got anything to drink? Can I have this last can of soda?"

"Help yourself," Beth said as she lay back down on the sofa, pulling the blanket back over her and the dog.

He opened the can and took a few sips before re-joining her in the living room. "I stopped across to the barn and said hello to Gabriel. He and his brother are pretty busy in there. I think he said they had a large order to get out next week, so they'll be working around the clock. I love the smell of sawed lumber, don't you?"

"Uh-huh," she responded, her eyes glued to the television.

"So, are you not feeling well?" he asked.

"I feel fine. Why do you ask?"

He shrugged. "I don't know, maybe because you're still in your pajamas."

Beth frowned. "I like my pajamas and I'm comfortable. I don't comment on the way you look, do I?"

She was beginning to understand why her brother had come to see her.

"How long have you had that bathrobe? I remember you had that thing when you were still living at home. Maybe it's time you retire that thing."

Beth quickly sat up. "Have you come to critique my wardrobe or are you going to tell me why you're here?"

His face serious, he answered her. "I'm here because your husband is worried about you. I'm here because the last time you spent 3 days in that bathrobe, you had the flu. Now, unless you have the flu or are physically sick, something else is wrong."

"Can't I have a few days of doing nothing? Since I went off to college and law school after that, I've done nothing but study and work. So what if I'm taking a few mental health days to do nothing. I've earned that right."

Christopher waited a few minutes before continuing. His voice soft and calm, he added, "Yeah, but you haven't earned the right to stink up the place. When did you last take a shower?"

A burst of laughter from Beth meant that her closest sibling had done what he'd come to do. Christopher gave Beth something to laugh about, and that had more value than junk food and tv binge-watching.

"I'd come over and hug you, but I'm afraid of the stench. Why don't I stay sitting over here and you tell me what's going on? I've got all the time in the world."

She wanted to cry but stayed composed and fought back tears.

"I don't know what's wrong. I really don't. I'm frustrated that I've worked for years at something that I shouldn't have. Remember how Lauren used to say that I'm a real Gemini because I can't make a decision to save my life? That's how this feels. It feels like when I finally did make the choice to go to law school and become a lawyer, I screwed up. I should have taken a different road, and now I'm nowhere."

"Wait a minute," he said. "You are not nowhere. Yeah, maybe you picked the wrong career...big deal. That doesn't mean there wasn't any value in what you learned. Every single day that we're alive on this earth, we're learning and growing. Even if the steps we take feel like we're going backward, we're not going backward."

Beth's eyes watered.

He continued, "You're uncomfortable because you took a predictable path. That's what law school does, right? And, now, that doesn't feel right to you. Don't beat yourself up about that because our lives are not linear. Our paths are all over the place to get us where we end up. That's called living. Look at me for example. Do you really think my plan was to get my leg blown off? I'm walking around with a prosthetic because of something I had no control over. Do I wish I never joined the military? Absolutely not. I'd do it all over again because that was something I wanted more than anything. So much so that I was willing to die for my country."

"Oh, Chris. You should be proud of the life you've built."

"I am proud. I never would have the career I have now if I hadn't lost my leg. I love working with these kids. I never would have known about them if this didn't happen to me. You're going to find your passion and your reason for getting up in the morning. I promise you. You *will* find it."

Beth jumped off the sofa, ran to her brother, and hugged him. "I love you, Chris. Thanks for coming to see me. I mean it. You really are helping me."

"Of course. It's what us Wheelers do, right? What did you say? We're in each other's business all the time? Weren't you in mine when I came home from the hospital? I don't know what I would have done if you weren't there for me.

"Listen, I've got to get back home before Becca gets out of work. Are you going to be ok?"

Beth nodded. "I'll be fine. I might still need a few more days of

Hallmark movies though. I don't know what it is about them but they are soothing, even if the storylines are all the same."

Christopher got up and took a few more gulps of his soda.

"Mind if I take this home with me?"

"It's yours. Say hello to Becca from us, will you?"

He got to the front door and turned. "Will do, and for heaven's sake, get rid of that bathrobe."

CHAPTER 13

The church hall was packed, with every chair taken. Lauren found seats for her family toward the back of the room. Olivia and Lilly ran over to see friends they knew from school.

Jeff nudged Lauren. "See what I mean? They've got a lot of friends here."

Irritated, Lauren sighed. "You promised to listen with an open mind, remember?"

Jeff shrugged and looked around the room. "Give me a break. How many people here do you think are thinking about doing what this family did? Isn't it possible that they're just here to be entertained? When I said I'd listen with an open mind, what I meant is that I'm willing to hear what they went through. That doesn't translate to me wanting to do the same thing."

Her frustration and impatience with Jeff growing, Lauren wondered whether her desire to do more for her children would eventually take a toll on her marriage. They'd already had one separation. Was she risking another?

"Good evening, everyone. The Trainor family can't wait to share their experience with you. We've had lots of questions about everything they went through, so eventually we thought it best you hear it directly from them. Just as a reminder, we'll have refreshments in the back as soon as their presentation is over. Every member of the Trainor family will answer your questions at the end of the video. That includes their children, so if any of the children here tonight have a question, go right ahead and ask. So, without further ado, we'll get the video started."

The lights were lowered and the room immediately went quiet as the video began.

The video presentation lasted about twelve minutes, starting with the family packing up and renting their home in Andover, to every stage of the move to Puerto Vallarta, Mexico. The family first flew to California and then Mrs. Trainor and the children flew to Mexico while Mr. Trainro bought a new car and drove to Mexico to meet up with the rest of his family. They explained enrolling their children in a bilingual school, how they stayed in a temporary rental until their final home was ready, and even broke down the cost of every part of their move.

At the end of the video there was a question and answer period where a surprising number of families wanted more detail on how they, too, might move to Mexico.

Jeff took the opportunity to ask his question as Lauren held her breath. "Was everyone in the family on board with this move? I mean, at any time did any of you think that maybe you were making a mistake?"

Jeff's question made it clear what his position was. Not only to Lauren, but for anyone in the room who cared to pay attention.

"Absolutely. My wife and I both worried we were crazy to do this. Not at the same time, though. One day I was doubtful and then when I thought it was a great idea, she changed her mind. We went back and forth about this for about six months before we finally were on the same page."

Jeff had a follow-up question. "Was there something that convinced the two of you to agree?"

Mr. Trainor wasted no time in answering. "What we did was give ourselves a time limit. We agreed to a six-month period of time away. If, by the end of six months, we had doubts or weren't on the same page, we'd come home. As you can see we stayed for one year, and we're glad that we did. The last six months were the best of our time there."

When the meeting was over and refreshments were consumed, they drove home in silence. It wasn't until they were almost home before Olivia spoke up. "That was really cool."

Lilly agreed. "I liked the lemon cake the best."

Lauren started to laugh. "What about the movie? What did you think of that family moving to Mexico for a year?"

"I thought it was interesting. Mallery Jenkins in my class stayed in England for a bunch of months. I think her grandfather was sick and so they all lived there for a while. He died though and she came back to school."

Jeff asked the most important question of the night. "Would you and Lilly like to move to another country for a while?"

'Maybe for the summer. I'm going to middle school in September so I wouldn't want to miss that. I pick Australia."

Lilly followed that up with her own perspective. "Can we move away next summer? Jenny Rowan said they're getting a pool put in their backyard. She said I can come over and swim if I want."

Lauren sighed and not one more word was said on the subject for the rest of the night.

Maggie tiptoed down the stairs and walked through the garden. She navigated around the piles of lumber and debris from the construction site and headed for her early morning walk on the beach.

The tropical air clung to her skin and before she'd walked several yards, she removed her hat to let the wind cool her forehead. Anticipating the humid weather, she'd worn her swimsuit and beach cover-up instead of her usual shorts and t-shirt.

She loved watching the seagulls dip into the ocean to find food before the crowd of tourists took over the water. Their squawking, or what the fishermen called mewing, along with the waves reaching her toes were the only sounds she could hear.

This, she thought, was why she'd moved to Captiva. In these precious moments, Captiva belonged solely to her. These mornings were hers alone, and no matter where she'd traveled, nothing could rival the tranquility she felt in this spot. The island wasn't just her home, it was her refuge, a private sanctuary not to be shared with anyone.

And yet, she longed for her entire family to be by her side. Grateful that her daughter Sarah lived close, Maggie missed the rest of her children and grandchildren. When she allowed herself to feel the pain of their absence, it was hard not to give up the life she'd built on Captiva and fly back to a world of familiar comfort.

However, that comfort came at a price she was no longer willing to pay. Unapologetically, she'd reached her dream of living on Captiva Island, and hated the times when doubt would sneak back into her thoughts. Old behaviors and traumas popping back into her mind always startled her.

In those moments, Maggie would question her obsessive thinking. *Wait. I thought I'd dealt with this already? Why is fear and uncertainty dominating my thinking?*

Maggie pushed those thoughts away and threw off her cover-up. She ran to the water and dove, head first, into the ocean.

Accepting the feathered friends flying above, she floated on her back and watched them swoop down and up again. Grateful to share the sea with the gulls she turned and reached forward with each stroke, traveling farther and farther away from the Key Lime Garden Inn.

After a time, she'd return to her home and tend to her chores. For now, she'd stay in the water until she could return to the present and capture her place in the world once more.

Chelsea needed something but couldn't put her finger on what was bothering her. Whenever that happened she'd mosey over to the Key Lime Garden Inn for one of Maggie's scones and a cup of coffee.

When she reached the back porch of the inn, Maggie, her hair still wet from her swim, ran over from the carriage house.

"Look at you getting up so late. Did you just get out of the shower?" Chelsea asked.

Maggie had energy to spare. "Nope. I went for a swim first thing this morning."

Iris and Riley were already cleaning up the breakfast dining room table.

"Good morning, Maggie...Chelsea," Riley said.

Chelsea looked around the kitchen but didn't see a scone in sight. "What gives? No scones?"

Maggie shrugged. "Sorry, Chelsea. I didn't have it in me to bake this morning."

"No, no, no. This will not do. I came over here specifically to get my morning scone. What am I going to do now?"

Iris and Riley giggled from the sink. "Oh, I don't know, bake something yourself one of these days?"

"We made omelets this morning, Chelsea. We can make you one if you'd like," Iris said.

Chelsea marched over to the coffee pot and poured herself a

cup. "No, that's ok. I appreciate it though. At least someone cares that I don't starve."

Maggie rolled her eyes and got a cup for herself. "So, what's the latest with Jacqui and the search for a commercial property?"

"Last I heard Trevor is having one of his real estate people find something for her. Captiva might not be feasible which means she's going to have to compete with the galleries on Sanibel."

"Is Sanibel even a consideration?" Riley asked.

Chelsea shrugged. "At this point I think Jacqui will grab what she can. I really hope she can find a property on Captiva though."

Maggie joined Chelsea at the table. "There aren't as many vacant commercial properties on Captiva though. It's a small island. I can't think of one place, can any of you?"

"I can," Millie said, joining them. "One half of Linda St. James' downstairs newspaper business is more than enough square footage for a gallery."

"Millie's right. Linda's place takes up the whole block. I hadn't thought of that. I'm sure she'd consider renting out the other half of the building," Maggie added.

Chelsea wasn't so sure. "I don't know. Someone wanted to rent that place last year and she wouldn't do it. It's possible the reason was the type of business. I think it was a music store."

Maggie laughed. "Oh, no wonder. Can you imagine the noise coming out of that place? Linda would lose her mind."

Everyone laughed, but Chelsea worried about a bigger problem. "Listen, Millie. I know you're good friends with Linda but she can be..."

"Difficult?" Millie asked.

Chelsea nodded. "That's putting it mildly. She's known for sticking her nose in where it doesn't belong. It's possible that whatever business shares the real estate with her might not appreciate her constant intrusions."

"Not to mention that Jacqui isn't one to run away from

confrontation. The two of them under the same roof might be a bad idea," Maggie said.

"I have an idea," Chelsea said. "Why don't I run it by Jacqui first? If she's willing to entertain the idea, then I say we go to Linda and ask her. I wouldn't rule it out completely. I might add that if this all goes south, I'm blaming Maggie."

"Me? Why me?"

Chelsea took a sip of her coffee. "It's simple, my dear. If this turns out to be a disaster, it will be because I made a mistake letting Millie talk us all into this. I can't be held responsible for bad decisions when I've been deprived of my usual morning scone."

CHAPTER 14

 yron and Louise Jameson lived so close to Sanibel that one part of his property sat on the Captiva/Sanibel town line. He'd had a years-long dispute with anyone who'd listen to his story that he was a Captiva islander, born and raised whenever his lineage was disputed.

The Bubble Room bar was Byron's home away from home and it was there where he'd argue everything from the island being home to pirates in the 1800s to the Wightman family's purchase of the property now known as The Mucky Duck.

The 'Tween Waters Inn opened during the Great Depression, and to hear Byron talk about it one would think he'd been alive during that time.

Now, in his early seventies, Byron seemed to see himself as the island's Mayor and authority on everything having to do with its future. With only the best intentions, Byron was considered a good person and in most things as a supporter of its year-round residents.

Lately, however, he'd kept close to home to care for his terminally-ill wife. Very few knew of their struggles, which was unusual considering Byron's obsessive need to discuss his personal life with anyone who'd listen.

Maggie now understood better the relationship between Byron and the residents of the island. What she couldn't understand is what would put him at odds with her and her family. The only way to find out was to visit him and Louise.

"Maggie!" Byron was surprised to see her standing at his front door.

"Hello, Byron."

"This is a surprise," he said.

"I'm sorry to barge in on you like this, it's just that we haven't seen you around town much lately and I was worried."

"Yes, well…"

"May I come in?" she asked hoping he wouldn't ask her to leave.

"Yes, I'm sorry. Please, come in."

He moved aside and opened the door and as Maggie passed over the threshold, she saw Louise in the living room. She lay in a hospital bed, a Hospice nurse sitting next to her.

"She's sleeping now," he whispered. "Perhaps it's best if we go to the back of the house. The nurse is here so she won't be alone."

"Would you like something to drink?" he asked as they sat in chairs on the back porch.

"No. Thank you. I'm fine. Byron, I don't know what to say. I've only found out about Louise just the other day. I'm truly sorry."

He nodded. "Thank you, Maggie. I appreciate you coming here today. I've been wanting to talk to you too, but…well, my focus has been on keeping Louise comfortable. Besides, I didn't know how to explain my actions."

"Your actions?" she asked, knowing full well what he was talking about.

"Aww, you know me. I'm always spouting off about one thing or another. I'm sorry if I seem petty in my complaining. Louise told me to go see you and apologize and I was going to…but… well, I didn't know how to explain."

"Byron, I don't mean to be dense, but perhaps you should explain. I'm not sure what it is that you're apologizing for."

He looked embarrassed as he continued. "Louise and I were really looking forward to your children's double wedding. We just assumed that we were going to get an invite. Louise even bought a new dress. She looked real pretty in it. Anyway, when the invitation didn't come, and then…well, Louise got sick. I don't know, I guess I lost my head. I got loud at The Bubble Room and started yelling about it. I even got thrown out of the place…first time that ever happened."

Maggie didn't want to laugh, but Byron seemed genuinely shocked at the establishment's reaction to his behavior.

"I've been a regular patron of that place for more than twenty years."

Maggie kept her composure. "I'm so sorry, Byron to both you and Louise. There was so much confusion with both weddings and I'm sure I didn't handle things the way I should have. There's no excuse for leaving you and Louise off the invitation list. Will you forgive me?"

"Of course I forgive you. I hope you'll forgive me too."

Maggie smiled. "Don't worry about anything. I'll explain everything to Paolo. I'm sure we can get the construction back on track quickly."

Byron looked confused. "The construction?"

"Yes, Michael Saccone sent a cease and desist letter telling us that we didn't explain properly what we were building. You know…the small cottage and cabana at the back of our property?"

Byron shook his head. "I knew about you guys building something back there, but that's all I know. Michael never said anything to me about sending you a letter."

Shocked at hearing this, Maggie got up out of her chair. "You mean you had nothing to do with stopping the construction because you were upset with us?"

Byron jumped out of his chair. "What? Oh my…no. I had nothing to do with…"

He stopped mid-sentence and put his hand to his mouth. "Oh no."

"What is it?"

"Michael was with me when I was complaining about not getting invited to the weddings. He's Louise's brother, you know."

Maggie nodded. "Yes, I've heard. Do you suppose in his desire to defend you and Louise, he might have stopped our project?"

Byron shrugged. "I suppose it's possible. He never said a word to me about it but I guess he wouldn't want Louise to know. Even in her state, she'd give him a real talking to. Michael loves his sister. He's a good man, just a bit impulsive. I can talk to him if you'd like."

"Oh, Byron, would you? I know it would relieve Paolo's anxiety."

"Of course. I'll find out what's going on and let you know just as soon as I can."

The Hospice nurse came out to the porch to find them. She looked at Byron and then Maggie.

"Louise is asking for you."

"I'll be right in," he said.

"No. Not you. She would like to see her," she said pointing to Maggie.

"Me?"

The nurse nodded.

Maggie looked at Byron, who was smiling. "That's my girl. She knows everything that's going on."

Maggie laughed and followed the nurse into the living room.

"Maggie," Louise said. "Thank you so much for coming to see me. I'm sorry I was sleeping when you got here."

The nurse left them alone as Maggie pulled a chair close to Louise.

"We've missed you down at the beach," she said to the dying woman.

Louise put her hand to her face and smiled. "No more tan for me."

Maggie took her hand. "That's ok. You still look beautiful."

Her voice softening, Louise looked into Maggie's eyes. "Do me a favor, will you? Will you and your family look after Byron when I'm gone? He's not very good at being alone."

"Of course we will," Maggie said, trying not to cry.

"I know how he can be, but he's a good man. He's got a good heart. We should have had children. They would have helped him now."

Maggie tapped her hand. "Don't you give it another thought. You and Byron are part of the Key Lime Garden Inn family. Not to mention, he's practically the island's Mayor. He won't be alone. I promise you."

"Thank you, Maggie. I've asked my brother Michael and his wife to keep an eye on him as well, but I know how much he loves your family."

Maggie suddenly felt that she needed to apologize to Louise for the wedding oversight.

"Louise, I'm so sorry for the wedding mix-up. Please know that if I'd had my wits about me, we would have invited you and Byron to the wedding. I don't know what I was thinking."

"Oh, my goodness. Did he complain to you about that again? I swear...that man."

Maggie shook her head. "No. He didn't. He apologized for being upset and possibly hurting our feelings. I truly didn't know anything about this until recently. Everything is fine now that we talked about it."

Louise closed her eyes and Maggie could tell that she struggled to stay awake.

"Louise, I think I'll go now and let you rest," she whispered. "I'll come back soon."

Louise didn't respond and the Hospice nurse, along with Byron returned to the living room.

Maggie kept her cool and wouldn't let the tears fall, but Byron wasn't as strong. He leaned into Maggie, put his head on her shoulder, and wept.

Maggie wasn't the same after speaking with Louise. She couldn't bring herself to tell Paolo about her meeting. She didn't want to talk about such unimportant things as the cabana construction and her husband's frustration over its delay.

Unable to share what was on her mind with anyone, she left the Jamesons' house and walked with no particular destination in mind. She was halfway to Sanibel when Chelsea's car pulled up alongside her.

"You lost?" she joked.

Maggie stopped walking and stood frozen on the sidewalk. She was angry and she didn't have a clue what she was angry about. "I needed to walk," she said, rubbing her jaw.

"You want me to keep going and pretend I didn't see you?"

Maggie nodded and Chelsea started to pull away.

Changing her mind, Maggie yelled, "Wait! Are you going home or somewhere else?"

"I was headed to Jerry's market for a few things. Do you want to come with me?"

Maggie got into Chelsea's car. "I don't want to go home."

"Okay," Chelsea said. "Do you want to tell me what's got you so upset?"

Maggie shook her head but said nothing.

They drove to the market in silence. When they reached the market, Maggie followed Chelsea inside and picked up a basket.

Without thinking, Maggie randomly selected items from the bakery, the produce section, and met Chelsea at the register.

Maggie's anger unabated, she slammed the car door when they got back inside.

"Okay, that's about all I'm going to take. You're going to tell me what's wrong and I'm not leaving this parking lot until you do."

Maggie looked out the window and shook her head. "I don't get it. I don't understand why humans learn nothing. We just keep doing the same things over and over again."

Chelsea shrugged. "I have no idea what you're talking about so give me an example."

"It's just that we get upset over the stupidest and unimportant things. Paolo has been miserable ever since Ciara's wedding. Then, to make matters worse, he's now upset about the construction even though he knows about Louise dying. Why do people have to wait until the world is falling around them before they recognize what's important? This construction project can just go away for all I care. It's not that important."

Maggie's eyes watered and she was ranting in such a way that she was having trouble breathing.

Chelsea opened up the brown paper bag from the market and dumped the contents onto the floor of the car. She handed Maggie the bag. "Here, breathe into this. Calm down and take slow breaths."

Maggie did as Chelsea instructed. For several minutes she breathed into the bag to reduce her hyperventilation. When she was relaxed, Chelsea took Maggie's hand.

"Do you want to tell me what's really going on? Is this about your scans coming up next month?"

Maggie nodded. "It's not that I'm scared my cancer is back. It's that even after everything I've gone through, Paolo still gets upset over things that really don't matter. Do you realize how much I don't sweat the small things anymore? That's the lesson our mortality teaches us. Instead of seeing that, he's acting like a petulant child."

Chelsea smiled. "Honey, he's human. Human beings are flawed. Trust me, Paolo knows what's important. It's just that he wants so badly for you to be proud of him. That's why he's working so hard to make that cottage and cabana perfect. He wants it perfect for you."

"Proud of him? How can he not know how much I admire everything he does?"

"I'm sure he knows that. But, that love and admiration you give him is addictive. He wants more of it so he keeps jumping through hoops to impress you."

Maggie felt foolish for not recognizing Paolo's motives. More to the point, she was astonished that her best friend did.

"You always know how to get right to the heart of things, Chelsea. Thank you for being such a good friend."

"Aww, you're pretty great yourself," Chelsea answered.

Maggie looked down at the floor of the car and the assortment of chocolate and candy. She looked up at Chelsea and laughed.

"You drove all the way to Jerry's to get candy?"

Chelsea shrugged and began collecting the boxes, putting them back into the paper bag.

"What can I say? I can't get this stuff anywhere else. Make fun of me all you want. If I didn't come along when I did, you'd probably have passed out on the side of the road from having a panic attack."

Maggie continued to laugh. "Give me a piece. I want to see what's so special about this life-saving candy."

CHAPTER 15

*B*eth tried to ignore the distance between her and Gabriel, but with it growing by the day, she had to do something. To her, Gabriel used his business as an excuse for not being available in her time of need. And, it was her opinion that he stayed in the barn much longer than usual, taking his dinner there, only coming back to the house when it was time for bed.

Frustrated, she took a shower, got dressed and marched over to the barn. Gabriel and his brother James were lifting a large armoire they had been working on for the last week.

Protected by safety glasses, their eyes focused on the task and didn't notice Beth until she cleared her throat.

"Oh, hey Beth," James said.

"Hi James. Gabriel, can I see you up at the house for a minute?"

James looked at Gabriel. "Go ahead. I need a break anyway."

Gabriel nodded, took off his glasses and followed Beth to the house. Their dog, Charlie, sat on the front porch and his tail beat against the wooden floor as Gabriel approached.

"Hey, Charlie," Gabriel said as he bent down and patted the dog's head.

Once inside, Beth didn't waste any time getting to her concerns.

"Why won't you fight with me?"

"Huh? What would you like me to fight with you about?"

"Don't play dumb. You know what I'm talking about. You're frustrated with me because I spend my days watching tv in my pajamas."

"Frustrated? Is that how you think I feel?"

"How would I know? You won't talk to me about anything."

Gabriel ran his hands through his hair and paced the floor. "Let me get this straight. You've been out of work and sitting at home for almost two weeks now. I've been here all this time, but you thought it was a good idea to have this conversation while I'm in the middle of working with my brother?"

Beth's voice rising, she didn't care if James heard them.

"When would there be a good time to talk, Gabriel? It's not like when James goes home we can talk then. You stay in the barn after he leaves, you eat your dinner there and don't come back inside the house until it's bedtime. I'm sure you'll say it's because of this big order that you have to fill, but it's more than that, and you know it. Talk to me."

"What can I say to you that I haven't already said, Beth? I'm supportive of your need to quit your job and find something else that makes you happy. It's just that you don't seem to be doing anything toward that end. I feel like when I look into your eyes, there's nothing there. I don't care what you do for a living as long as the spark that I love returns. I don't think you're going to find what you're looking for sitting on the sofa watching television all day."

Beth knew Gabriel was right, but she was lost as to what to do about it.

He walked to her and wrapped his arms around her, pulling her into him.

"Come back to me, Bethy," he whispered.

She buried her head in the crook of his neck and tried not to cry.

He took her hand and they walked to the sofa. "Listen, I've got an idea. You've got another week on your paid time off. Why don't you go down to Captiva to see your mother?"

Beth shook her head. "No. I'm not running to Mommy."

"Hear me out. The day Christopher came by something inside you lit up. There was a change in your mood. It was subtle but I could tell that his visit helped you some. Bethy, you get your strength from your family. It's pretty incredible the way you and siblings seem to complete each other. I'm close with my brother, but what you and your family have is something else. I think a week on Captiva Island is what you need."

Beth knew in her heart that Gabriel was right, but she didn't know how to deal with feeling like a failure. Going to see her mother might make her feel better, but then again, it might not.

"I'll think about it," she said. "I'm sorry I dragged you away from work. I know you're busy. It's just I couldn't take the silence anymore."

He nodded. "I understand that. Please consider Captiva. I promise you that between your mother, Sarah, Chelsea and your grandmother, you'll have plenty of advice to consider."

Beth smiled. "That's a good thing?"

Gabriel laughed. "For me it would be awful, but for a Wheeler it's like getting IV fluids when you're dehydrated."

Beth chuckled at how accurate he was about her family. It was up to her whether she was willing to grab onto the Wheeler life-line and save herself from uncertainty. Beth was drowning and although Gabriel couldn't save her, he was wise to send her to the people who could.

Sarah put a beach blanket out on the sand and looked at her watch. Emma and her sister Jillian were due to arrive for a day at the beach and girl time while Trevor, Finn and Gareth went golfing.

Debbie, their part-time nanny, took the children to the zoo so that Sarah and her friends could talk uninterrupted.

Sarah heard the car doors shut and had instructed her guests to come around to the back of the house to find her.

"Hey, we're here," Emma said.

"Yay. I'm so glad you guys could come."

"You are so lucky to have this property, Sarah," Jillian said. "If I lived on the beach like this, I don't think I'd ever go to work."

Emma laughed, "Oh yes you would. You can't stand to be away from your patients."

Jillian nodded. "I guess you're right about that."

"I think it's wonderful that you love being a veterinarian. I love animals myself, but I don't think I could go through all the education to get there. It's just like being a doctor for humans, isn't it?"

"It sure is and thank you for saying that. You have no idea the perception that it's much easier to go through medical school for veterinary training. It's still quite difficult and takes serious commitment."

"Which is why Jillian is struggling to figure out where to live these days," Emma added.

"Emma!" her sister yelled. "Don't make a big deal out of this."

"What? You can tell Sarah. She's my best friend."

"What are we talking about?" Sarah asked.

"Finn Powell is staying on the east coast for work. I'm in Naples so it's about a three and a half hour drive to see each other. This has been going on for almost a year, and it's not been easy. Between his flying and my practice, we can't see each other very much," Jillian said.

"Finn wants her to open up a practice on the east coast," Emma explained.

"Can you afford to do that?" Sarah asked.

"That's a good question. I'm not sure, but more to the point is that's a major commitment for both my business *and* our relationship. I'm not sure I'm ready for that."

Sarah nodded. "That certainly makes sense. I can understand your reluctance." Sarah took things further. "If you don't mind my saying so, you and Finn seem very much in love."

Jillian smiled. "You're right about that. I'm not sure why I'm hesitating."

"I do," said Emma. "Ever since Jillian was a kid, she insisted that she was never going to get married. She'd date a guy and maybe even convince herself that she was in love, but within a few months, she was over him."

Jillian punched her sister's arm. "That's not true. Well, it's not entirely true. Here's the thing, I'm terrified of commitment. Trust me, it took a lot for me to open my clinic, and nothing gives me more happiness than caring for animals. I literally panic at being trapped in something from which I can't escape."

"That's how you feel about Finn, that you're trapped?"

Jillian shook her head. "I'm not now, but if I move to the east coast..."

"Ah, I see. Here's the thing, Jillian, and I really believe this. I think when you've found the right person, something else kicks in. I don't know how to explain it except to say that all doubt falls away. I don't mean worrying about whether things will go well or whether you'll be good at something. I mean that you don't have one second of a doubt about the person."

"Listen to her, Jilly. Sarah is a perfect example of this. She never wanted to get married...never wanted children. Now, look at her. She's married with three children and put off working outside the home so she could be with her kids as they grow."

Sarah nodded. "It's true. I was the poster girl for never marrying...never motherhood, but when I fell in love with Trevor...oh my goodness. I was gone...completely gone. Then, when Sophia was left at my door as an infant, I was in love for life."

"Not only that, but Trevor was also a father already. Sarah married Trevor, adopted both Sophia and Noah, and then they had little Maggie last year," Emma added.

"I can't tell you what to do about Finn, but I can tell you that, for me, in an instant I found that I couldn't live without Trevor and Noah. When they came into my life, I wanted to be in theirs forever."

"You never doubted your choices?" Jillian asked.

"Oh, I worried that I wouldn't be a good enough mother. After all, I was a fairly good aunt to my nieces, but being a mother was completely new territory for me. Noah's mother wasn't in the picture at all, so I had to step up and be a full time mother to him if Trevor and I wanted a future together. After a while, I realized that it would take time for all of us to adjust, but our love for each other is what made all of it possible."

Sarah could see that watching Jillian's internal struggle was difficult for Emma. The sisters were close, and nothing was harder than feeling helpless while a loved one wrestled with unanswered questions.

"You'll figure it out, Jillian," Sarah said. "When do you go back home?"

"Not for another week. I've taken this time off not only for the wedding in Italy, but to spend some time with Emma... and Gareth of course. I still can't believe my big sister is married."

Sarah smiled. "See? She's another perfect example of someone who never planned to marry." She winked at her best friend. "The next thing you know, she'll be buying a house in Florida and having babies."

"Bite your tongue," Emma said. "I'm an award-winning

National Geographic photographer for heaven's sake. My feet will never be planted firmly anywhere for long."

Sarah laughed at that while secretly praying Emma would change her mind. She'd never share her dream with her friend but nothing would make Sarah happier than to have her children grow up alongside Emma's.

CHAPTER 16

*M*aggie couldn't wait any longer. Enough time had passed, and Paolo was aware of the Jameson's situation. There was no reason to get upset or storm off to confront Michael Saccone. She'd explain as calmly as possible and insist that Paolo let Byron handle things.

"Got a minute?" she asked, watching Paolo finish stacking the palm fronds in the corner.

"Just barely. I've got to get over to Sanibellia. What's up?"

"It seems that it was Louise's brother, Michael Saccone, who pulled the building permit."

"What? Why for heaven's sake?"

"I guess Byron was with him at the Bubble Room bar and had a few too many. He was extremely upset with us for him and Louise not getting invited to the double wedding. He said that Louise had bought a new dress and was really looking forward to it. At the bar, he was spouting off for everyone to hear. It seems that her brother was just as upset for Louise more than anything."

"I understand their feelings, but Maggie, that's unprofessional at best and downright petty."

Maggie nodded. "Of course it was but what does that matter

now? Are you going to confront a man who is grieving? Byron didn't know anything about this. He said that he'd handle it, but honey, we can't put a timetable on this. We're going to have to let Byron do what he will in his own time. The cabana and cottage will just have to wait."

Lexi bounced around the fenced-in area that Paolo had constructed for her protection. The little pup reached the half-built cabana and kept trying to climb over the lower part of the frame. On her third attempt she made it over and ran to Paolo, jumping into his arms.

The timing was perfect. Paolo smiled at his new best friend and then shrugged and smiled.

"Okay. I guess there's nothing we can do about it now. I think I'll take Lexi with me to Sanibellia. I want her to try out her new car seat anyway."

He kissed Maggie's cheek and walked out of the garden and toward the inn.

Maggie couldn't believe that Lexi had saved the day once more.

Lauren stared at the computer screen. Two newly sold homes were reason to celebrate, but her mind was focused on other things.

She placed her hand on her growing belly and smiled. She couldn't wait to meet her baby. With only two more months to go in her pregnancy, she was excited to hold a newborn in her arms once again.

Her thoughts about moving her family out of the country pushed aside, she felt a strong urge to make changes in ways that she could control. Already decorated with hues of gray and yellow, the nursery was nearly ready and her desire to nest was strong.

Her cellphone buzzed on her desk and she picked it up and hit the unmute button. "Hey, Beth. This is a surprise. You hardly ever call me at work. What's new with you?"

"Oh, not much, only that my entire world has fallen apart."

Lauren snickered. "Yup, that's my dramatic little sister. Does Gabriel know that his wife's world has fallen apart or hasn't he been told?"

"Trust me, he knows and has what he considers to be the solution."

"Oh?" Lauren asked.

"He thinks I need to go to Captiva and see Mom."

Lauren sat up straight in her chair. "Okay, you've got my attention. Things must be pretty terrible for Gabriel to suggest that. What's going on?"

"I'm seriously thinking of quitting my job. More specifically, leaving the District Attorney's office completely."

"What? Why? You've worked so hard to get where you are in your career."

"I know that Lauren, but it's not what I want. It's difficult to explain. All I know is that I'm struggling and I need time to figure out what I'm going to do. Mitchell's giving me three weeks paid time off and it's already been two weeks. I'm going out of my mind and I'm driving Gabriel crazy too. Although, he's being really sweet about it all."

Lauren always felt that Beth wasn't cut out to be a prosecuting attorney. Beth was a strong woman, but too much of an empath to deal with the violence and despair on the city streets.

"What are you going to do?"

"I've decided to go to Captiva. I need to talk to Mom. I want to see Sarah and Grandma too, and I want you to come with me."

"Me? Why do you need me?"

"I want you to come because I want all us Wheeler women to be together. Becca and Brea can't come because of school and work so I'm not even going to bother to ask them. I want my big sisters with me. Please say you'll come?"

Lauren kept the recent confusion and anxiety about her family to herself. Having put her concerns about her children's education aside, she wondered if a talk with her mother might shed light on what to do next.

"You know, I think I could use a little of Grandma's words of wisdom. I miss Mom and Sarah too. Count me in. When do you want to go?"

"How about tomorrow? I can book our flight as soon as I hang up."

"Tomorrow? Beth, I have to tell Jeff and the girls that I'm leaving. I don't know about this."

"Lauren, I don't have that much time before I have to decide. Mitchell isn't going to wait forever. I've already lost time watching tv in my pajamas."

"Fine. I better go. I need to get home and pack. Send me the flight info when you get it and let me know how much I owe you for the ticket. I'll meet you at the airport. I can't believe we're going to Captiva. You'd better call Mom and let her know."

"I will. I'm going to call her right after I hang up with you. Thanks Lauren. I mean it. You're the best sister in the world."

Lauren laughed. "Really? Well, you better remember that next time I need a favor."

<hr />

Beth decided to call her sister Sarah before placing a call to her mother. It wasn't that she was afraid to tell her mother that she was quitting her job, she thought it best to first get Sarah's support. The more confident Beth felt about her decision the easier it would be to answer her mother's questions.

Famous for her devil's advocate position, Maggie Moretti could be downright incisive when asked for her opinion. Beth wasn't sure she wanted her mother's opinion as much as she wanted her to listen and support her decision. Whatever the outcome, Beth needed to be prepared for her mother's reaction.

"You did what?" Sarah yelled into the phone.

"I haven't *done* anything yet. All I've done is take a few weeks off."

"A technicality, Beth. You and I both know you will quit the minute you get back home. Be straight with me. Are you quitting or taking a trip to Florida to get Mom to talk you out of it?"

"Okay, you're right and wrong. I am going to quit when I get home and I want my family's support. Is that too much to ask?"

Beth sounded angry, which was not how she wanted this phone call to go. "I'm sorry. I didn't mean to raise my voice. It's just that this will be a huge transition for me and I need my family during this difficult time."

Beth could tell that Sarah stayed silent to let her rant. But, after a few seconds, she spoke again. "Are you done?"

"I think so," Beth answered.

"Okay then this is what I think you should say to Mom. I think that if you're truly certain this is what you are going to do, then you stay strong and emphatic. Tell her what you just told me. You know she'll support whatever makes you happy. We all will."

"Thanks, Sarah. That's all I need to hear. I'm going to call Mom right now. Wish me luck?"

"You'll be fine. Text me when you've landed tomorrow okay? I can't wait to see you and Lauren. Safe travels."

"Will do. Love you, Sis."

"Love you too."

Ciara and Crawford arrived home from their honeymoon and stopped into the Key Lime Garden Inn to see Paolo and Maggie.

Paolo's face lit up when they came through the back door.

"Hey, everyone. We're home."

"Hey, how was the honeymoon?" Maggie asked as Paolo kissed his sister.

"Incredible," Crawford answered. "Next to Gaeta, I think I loved Venice the most. It's just so different from any other city in Italy."

Ciara laughed. "The truth is that I think Crawford's favorite thing was all the delicious food."

He shrugged. "She's right. I'm afraid to get on the scale. I bet I gained ten pounds on this trip. How is everyone here? Anything new on the island?"

Millie joined them in the kitchen.

Riley and Iris laughed. "Are you kidding? A day doesn't go by when there isn't something new happening. Riley's got a new boyfriend," Millie said.

"Millie! Why don't you announce it to the whole island?" Riley lamented.

"Oh, come on, Riley. Everyone on the island already knows about you and Andrew."

"Gee, I wonder why that is?" Iris added.

Looking at Riley, Ciara beamed. "That's exciting news. You'll have to tell me all the details."

Just then, little Lexi came barreling through the kitchen carrying a new toy in her mouth.

"Who is this?" Ciara asked.

Paolo picked the dog up and cradled her in his arms. "This is Lexi. We adopted her when we got back from Italy."

"Your brother is madly in love with this little fur baby," Maggie said.

"Hello, Lexi," Ciara said, taking the dog from Paolo. "I'm your Aunt Ciara and this is your Uncle Crawford."

Ciara cuddled the pup but the dog seemed more interested in Crawford. Backing away, he said, "I'm not very good with animals. Somehow they don't seem to care and want to get close to me anyway."

Maggie looked down at her cellphone.

"It's Beth," she said.

"Tell her we all say hello," Paolo added.

Maggie walked out the back door and sat on the porch swing. "Hi, honey. I'm so glad you called. How are you and Gabriel?"

"We're fine. How are things down there?"

"Busy, but good. Your step-father has a girlfriend though. Her name is Lexi and she has four legs."

"Mom, you didn't? You got a dog?"

"We did. Paolo's been wanting one forever and so when we got back from Italy we figured the time was right. I wish you could see her, she's adorable."

"Well, I think that's going to happen. Lauren and I are coming down tomorrow."

"What? You're coming to Captiva?"

"Yup. I already called Sarah to let her know. We're taking the six AM flight."

"Well, do you want me to come pick you up?"

"No, I'd rather rent a car. I'm not sure how long I'm staying. Lauren might come back before me."

Maggie could feel something was off with Beth. Usually full of life and spunk, she sounded tired and vague about her plans.

"That's fine, honey. You know that you're welcome to stay here as long as you want. Are you sure everything is okay between you and Gabriel?"

"Everything's great between us. I just miss you, Sarah and Grandma. I asked Lauren to go with me because I thought it would be great to have a 'girls only' family get-together."

"That does sound like fun. Oh, honey, I'm so excited to see you two. I've got plenty of room. Summer in Florida isn't the best time to visit so we're not fully booked. Prepare yourself though, it's humid and we have downpour rain just about every after-noon like clockwork."

"I don't care if it snows. I just want to see you guys," Beth said. "Tell Grandma that we're coming will you?"

"Of course. I'll call her later today. She had some get-together with a bunch of women her age from Marina Bluffs."

"Great. Thanks, Mom. I'll see you tomorrow."

Maggie wasn't sure what all this was about but one thing she knew for certain. Her daughters weren't coming to Captiva just to vacation.

She walked into the kitchen. "Riley, make sure we have plenty of tea."

"You mean iced-tea?"

"Nope. I'm talking about my special tea leaves. Beth and Lauren are coming tomorrow. Looks like I might have a double whammy on my hands. I better keep my calendar open. My gut tells me I've got lots of listening coming up with these two. Now that I think of it, make sure we've got plenty of tissues too."

CHAPTER 17

*M*aggie poured herself a glass of iced tea and went back outside. She wasn't on the porch swing for more than five minutes when Sarah pulled her car up in front of the carriage house.

"You heard?" she said getting out of the car.

"I heard. I just hung up from Beth. You got over here in record time. How long ago did she call you?"

"About an hour ago. I wanted to see if you needed me to do anything or if you wanted them to stay with us."

Maggie laughed. "Are you kidding? You've got your hands full with the kids. We've got a couple of rooms available. Do you want iced tea?"

"No, thanks. I'm good. Do you need me to do anything or pick anything up at the store? I can check with Riley if you want."

"That's very sweet of you. I think we're good."

Sarah nodded. "Trevor's father went back to work today."

"Really? I didn't know he'd improved that much."

"Well, I can't say exactly what he can and can't do. He's got a cane so he has to get around slower than before obviously, but

I'm guessing he'll be sitting behind his desk barking orders just as he did before the stroke."

"How are the kids?"

"They're good. Debbie is at the house watching them. Having a part-time nanny has been a life-saver. Emma and Jillian came over the other day and we had a nice time out on the beach."

At any time in her children's lives, Maggie could spot deflection a mile away.

"Sarah, why don't you tell me what's going on with Beth?"

"I was hoping to see little Lexi. Where is she?"

"Paolo took her to Sanibellia. So it's not Beth…it's Lauren?"

"Mom, please don't put me on the spot like that. It's not my story to tell. All you have to do is wait one more day. Trust me, it's not the end of the world. No one is sick. So, rest easy. Do your mommy thing tomorrow…not today."

Maggie laughed. "My mommy thing? What is that?"

Sarah laughed. "You know what I'm talking about. The way you manage to squeeze information out of your children even when they don't want to tell you stuff."

"I don't do that," Maggie insisted.

"Right, I bet you got your special tea and teapot out of the cabinet already."

Maggie didn't make eye contact with Sarah.

"Looks like the apple doesn't fall far from the tree. I guess I taught you some of my magic. Soon, you'll be buying your own teapot and having nice long talks with your children."

Sarah rolled her eyes. "Don't rush things. I'm definitely not ready for that."

"Knock, knock," Millie said. "Linda, you around?"

"Come on in. I'm fighting with the printing machine," Linda

answered. "This thing is so old I don't even know why I'm still using it."

"Why don't you buy a new one?"

"Because they're super expensive, that's why. I've been putting this off for years but I think I don't have a choice now."

"I might have a solution for your printing troubles," Millie offered. "Why not rent out the rest of the commercial space? You could ask for a lot of money for that rental."

"That's the problem. Captiva is expensive. No one has the money to pay me what I'd want," Linda said.

"What if I know someone who might be interested?"

"You know someone who can afford to rent on Captiva?"

Millie nodded. "I do...Jacqui Hutchins. She wants to open an art gallery and has the financial backing to do it. She's having a hard time finding a place. There aren't many rentals on the island. Not commercial property anyway. I thought of your place the minute I heard she was looking. It would solve your printing problem and then some."

Linda stopped fussing with the printer and seemed to consider the possibility.

"How soon would she want to get in here? The place needs a lot of work. I mean I couldn't get it in shape for at least a couple of months."

"Are you kidding me? Jacqui is dating Joshua Powell who works just across the way from you. She's got Chelsea's support and everyone at the Key Lime Garden Inn would help. You could get this place up and running within a month if you're willing."

Linda nodded. "Bring her around tomorrow. Let's see if it's a good fit. I'm not the easiest person to get along with, you know."

Millie wanted to say that was an understatement but kept her mouth shut and tried not to laugh.

"I'll see you tomorrow. Thanks a bunch, Linda."

Millie raced out of Linda's place and headed straight across the street to Powell Water Sports. Crawford Powell was wiping down the glass case at the register when Millie walked in.

"Hey Crawford. Is Joshua around?"

"Hi Millie. Yes, he's out at the golf carts."

"Thanks," she said, running out the door.

She went to the side of the building where the golf cats were. When she found Joshua he was helping a customer. She waited patiently until he was done before approaching him.

"Hey, Millie. It's nice to see you. What brings you to Powell's?"

"Hi Joshua. I want to get a message to Jacqui as soon as possible. Can you send her a text from me?"

"Sure. What should I say?

"Tell her to be at Linda St. James' place at ten o'clock tomorrow morning. Tell her that Linda is considering renting out space for her art gallery."

Joshua stopped typing and looked up at Millie. "Are you serious? She's been adamant for years that she'd never rent it."

Millie beamed with pride. "I got her to change her mind. Just tell Jacqui to be there, okay?"

Joshua nodded. "Okay. Thanks, Millie."

Millie walked back to the Key Lime Garden Inn and couldn't wait for the next day. She'd accomplished something that no one else had been able to all these years.

Of course she couldn't say for certain that everything would work out, but she crossed her fingers as she walked down Andy Rosse Lane. Crossed fingers almost always worked for her in the past, and there was no reason to expect that it wouldn't work this time too.

"You've got to come with me. I'm not dealing with Linda St. James and Millie by myself. You know them better than I do anyway. Please say you'll come?" Jacqui pleaded.

Since Chelsea promised to support Jacqui she couldn't easily refuse her request.

"Of course I will. I'm stopping over to Maggie's first thing in the morning but I can be free any time after nine. What time did Millie say we should meet her?"

"Ten o'clock so that's perfect. Thank you so much, Chelsea. I'm so excited. I can't believe this might actually happen. Are you sure you won't come in on this with me?"

"I'm sure, honey. Remember what I said to you before? You can do this. Repeat those words every day until it happens."

The next morning Maggie was up before the sun and in the kitchen baking cranberry walnut scones and almond croissants. The heavenly smell from the kitchen welcomed the day and anyone within a half mile radius of the Key Lime Garden Inn. The pastry and coffee was ready as soon as Chelsea showed up at six in the morning.

"Good morning," Maggie whispered. "This is early even for you."

"Are you still baking or do we have time to walk the beach for a bit?"

"We've got time, let me turn off the stove."

They tiptoed out of the kitchen making sure not to slam the screen door. When they walked through the garden, Maggie realized something she'd never noticed before.

"Chelsea, look at this," Maggie said, pointing to the bench near the koi pond.

"What is it?"

"The initials. Do you see them?"

"Maggie, this bench has been covered in carvings since it was first put in this yard by Rose years ago."

"Of course I know that. That's not what I mean. Look at the letters in the corner with the heart around it."

"B.S.J. And L.E.S. That's Byron and Louise. It's got to be," Maggie said.

"Why would their letters be on this bench, I wonder?" Chelsea asked.

Maggie shook her head and then traced the letters with her fingers. She took out her cellphone and took a picture of the carving.

"I'll have to find out what their middle names are but I think Byron carved these letters when they were dating."

"Are you serious? That was forever ago. How old is this bench?"

Maggie shook her head. "No idea."

"It's not like we can't find out these details. First and foremost why not just go ask Byron, or better yet, have him come over and then you walk through the garden, see if he has any reaction to the bench? Let him talk first. If he doesn't take the bait, come right out and ask him."

They left the bench and headed toward the water.

"Isn't that just the sweetest thing?" Maggie asked. "I can't get over it. We've been sitting out here and the guests have been as well and it never occurred to us to find out its origins."

"Well, now's your chance," Chelsea said.

Maggie shook her head. "Not today it isn't, and maybe not even the rest of the week. Lauren and Beth are coming to the island. They should be here by one o'clock if everything goes well. I doubt I'm going to have much time to do more than spend it with my girls."

"You never mentioned Lauren and Beth were coming."

Maggie chuckled. "That's because I didn't know until yesterday afternoon. I don't think either of them had this planned much longer than that. I don't like it either. Something is wrong. They wouldn't be traveling here last minute like this if everything was fine."

"Why wouldn't they tell you on the phone?"

"Because they probably don't want me to worry. Sarah knows what this is all about although she won't tell me. I tried getting it out of her, but I had zero luck. To make matters worse, Beth told me to call my mother and let her know that they'd be here today and I completely forgot."

"Well, that was convenient."

Maggie laughed. "Stop it. I didn't do it on purpose, but I must admit, adding my mother into the mix isn't exactly a good idea, if you ask me. I need time alone with my daughters before my mother starts interfering."

They walked a good mile before turning back to walk another. "I think this is the most exercise I've had in weeks. Since Christmas I've really let myself go," Maggie said.

"Once upon a time you and I talked about getting regular exercise. I think we should commit to doing this every morning. What do you say?"

"I say if you really want to get healthy, you'll stop eating my scones and drinking my coffee."

"Why? Is there something wrong with them?"

"No, but some might say there's too much fat…too much butter. That increases your cholesterol."

"Maggie, it is far too early in the morning to be talking numbers to me. You know how bad I am with numbers. I'm a word person."

Maggie giggled. "Translation…you're good at talking a person's ear off."

"Nice, Maggie. You're such a good friend."

CHAPTER 18

*C*helsea excused herself when Michael Saccone personally delivered the new building permit to Paolo and Maggie. "I'll come by this afternoon. Text me when Lauren and Beth arrive."

Maggie nodded and walked to the driveway.

Byron accompanied Mr. Saccone and Maggie wondered if that was because he wanted to make sure the issue was resolved or to give his brother-in-law support.

"I'm not proud of the way I behaved, Mrs. Moretti. I hope you'll understand that I wasn't in my right mind," Michael said.

"Of course we understand," Maggie said. "These are stressful times for your family and all of us are only human. We make mistakes."

She wanted to apologize once again for not inviting them to the wedding, however she didn't want to open old wounds once again.

"Thank you for delivering this in person, Mr. Saccone. We appreciate it," Paolo said.

Michael Saccone nodded and got back in his car. Byron hugged Maggie and got into the car after him. As they drove off,

126

Maggie wondered if the next time she saw either of them would most likely be at Louise's funeral. Instinctively she turned and hugged Paolo. He held her tight and then went back to the garden to work.

Maggie then did what she'd promised Beth she'd do earlier but forgot.

Her mother answered her phone after only one ring. "Nice of you to remember your mother. I haven't heard from you since our lunch a couple of weeks ago. You know that I'm practically down the street from you now, right?"

Maggie rolled her eyes. Down the street wasn't exactly accurate given the fact that Maggie was on an island and it took almost an hour to get from Captiva to her mother's place.

"Sorry, Mom. As always, it's been a little busy here. I meant to call you earlier about this but the day got away from me. Beth and Lauren are flying down today. I expect they'll be here right after lunch. Would you like them to stop on their way and pick you up?"

"Oh dear. Had you called me earlier I would have been able to change my plans, but as it is, I won't be able to join you. I'm spending the day with several of the ladies in this part of the facility. Josie has a car and we all can fit in that."

"Where are you all going?"

"I'd tell you but you're so darn opinionated about the things I do. I hesitate to say anything."

Maggie now was worried that her mother was once again planning to do something for which she didn't approve.

"Mother, you can tell me. Where are you all going?"

"Well, if you must know. Doris admired my tattoo when we were playing cards. Next thing I knew she and the three other women I was playing with said they wanted a tattoo as well. Ellen Flaherty wanted to come with us but she's on blood thinners so she can't get a tattoo. Last thing I need is to kill one of these women. I don't want to get kicked out of the place."

"Mom, I really think you ought to pass on the tattoos. Tell these ladies that you can't go because your granddaughters flew down at the last minute. You don't know the health of these women. They could have high blood pressure or heart disease or another illness that would make getting a tattoo dangerous. You shouldn't take on that responsibility."

"Maggie dear, do you see what I mean? I can't tell you anything. They are perfectly within their right to make choices without consulting with you. You act as if they all have dementia. Well, Doris sometimes forgets to put her teeth in, but the rest of us are pretty sharp."

Maggie's concern grew by the minute. "Mom, please, do me a favor and cancel this. You want to see your granddaughters, don't you? They will be driving right by your place on their way here."

"How long will they be staying on Captiva?"

"I'm not sure, why?"

"Let's make plans for someone to come get me this week. We'll have a great time. In the meantime, I've got to go. Tell the girls I love them and will see them soon. And, Maggie, for heaven's sake, lighten up. Maybe before the girls go back up north we all could get matching tattoos. Wouldn't that be marvelous?"

It wasn't enough that Maggie's stress level was rising after her mother's phone call. To add to the chaos, Isabelle Barlowe stopped by the inn to say hello.

Maggie ran to the carriage house to slip inside before Isabelle saw her but was too late.

"Maggie!" she called out. "Oh, my friend. You have no idea how happy I am to see you. Sebastian and I just flew in from Paris last night. I'm exhausted. Tell me how have you been?"

Isabelle and Sebastian Barlowe lived on Captiva Island only part of the year. The rest of the time they spent in Paris.

They'd only been married a couple of years and Isabelle did her best to enjoy the beauty and nature Captiva offered, often creating drama for no reason other than that she was bored.

"Busy as usual. It seems as if that's how things are around here all the time. Today is no different. Two of my daughters are flying down to spend time with me. I've got so much to do before they get here. Maybe we can talk another time?"

"But of course. I love your family and will come to see them soon, oui?"

"Oui," Maggie responded, speaking one of the few French words she'd learned in school.

Isabelle walked down the driveway and out onto the road, no doubt to buy more clothes from one of the expensive Captiva shops nearby.

———

Jacqui and Chelsea walked to Linda's place and the anticipation was too much for Jacqui. "I'm so nervous. What if she doesn't like me or doesn't want me working so close to her?"

"Then you won't be any worse off than you are now. You've got nothing to lose and truthfully, neither does she. That spot has been left practically abandoned. It's an eye sore. You'll be doing her a favor turning it into an art gallery."

Both Linda and Millie were waiting outside the building when they approached.

"What's Millie doing here?" Jacqui asked.

"I have no idea. Probably sticking her nose in where it doesn't belong. Something that Linda does all the time. You'll have to get used to that."

"Linda, how are you?"

Linda nodded. "Chelsea. Nice to see you. I didn't know you were coming."

"Yes, well, Jacqui asked me to and I obliged. Jacqui, this is Linda St. James. I'm not sure that the two of you have ever met."

Jacqui shook Linda's hand. "Actually, we have. I was around a couple of summers ago staying at Chelsea's. She and I were painting together. I'm pretty sure you and I met once that summer."

Linda nodded. "You do look familiar. You're dating Joshua Powell I understand?"

Jacqui nodded. "Yes, we've been seeing each other for a while now."

"Why don't we go inside and you can look at the place. I'm not sure if the square footage is enough for your business."

Linda pushed several cobwebs aside as they entered the space. There were two large windows in the front facing the road, and a smaller one in the back. There was a bathroom that appeared to be shared with the town's newspaper business.

There was one large room and another smaller room but it was large enough for Jacqui's first gallery.

"Chelsea, what do you think?" Jacqui whispered.

"I think it could work. If the price is right."

"I like it. It needs work of course. I can do everything. You don't have to lift a finger if you don't want to. How much is the rent?"

"Sixteen hundred a month. Do you think you can afford that?" Linda asked.

Jacqui smiled. "No problem at all. I'll need to get working on the place as soon as possible. Would that be okay?"

"I'll need two months' rent up front. You say you don't need me to work with you on the place?"

Jacqui shook her head and looked across the road. "Nope. I've got plenty of help."

Beth ran into her mother's arms the minute she and Lauren reached the Key Lime Garden Inn. "I'm so happy to see you," Beth said.

Lauren joined them and all three stayed frozen in place in the middle of the driveway for some time.

"Let me look at you," Maggie said standing back admiring Beth's body. "You look healthy to me. You are healthy, right?"

Beth laughed. "It depends, are you talking mentally or physically? Physically, I think I could run a marathon, mentally...let's call it emotionally, I'm not so sure."

Maggie looked at Lauren, and then rubbed her daughter's belly.

"And, what about you? How are you and my little grandbaby doing?"

"We're fine, Mom. Everyone is fine."

"Okay, let's get you guys inside and have a little lunch. Have you eaten anything?"

"No, only the junk food on the plane," Lauren said.

"That's what I thought. Come inside, I had Riley and Iris prepare a few things. Chelsea had a meeting this morning but said she'd be by for lunch so I expect her any minute...Sarah too. Your grandmother wants to get together with you all sometime during your stay but not today. You won't believe the reason. She's taking a bunch of elderly women from Marina Bluffs to get a tattoo."

"No!" Beth screamed. "She isn't?"

"Oh yes she is," Lauren said. "I'm very familiar with that crazy woman. She's already got one tattoo. I'm worried that she's planning to get another. I don't think it's a good look for someone her age."

"Well, let me tell you, it's not only not a good look for these women, but it could be dangerous. One of the women who wanted to go is on blood thinners. Imagine that," Maggie explained. "Your grandmother has a habit of getting into trouble wherever she is. I'm just now realizing that because she moved down here, I'm going to have to keep my eye on her constantly."

"That's not easy considering she's quite a drive from here," Lauren added.

"The real point is that she's happy, right?" Beth asked.

Maggie nodded. "She is that."

Beth leaned down, picked up her luggage, and shrugged. "Then that's all that matters."

Maggie watched Beth go inside and then looked at Lauren. "Is someone going to tell me what's going on?"

Lauren put her arm around her mother's shoulders. "Give her time, Mom. She'll talk when she's ready."

CHAPTER 19

"Maggie, did you hear? Louise Jameson passed away," Millie said.

"What? When?"

"Last night. Linda told us this morning. I was with Chelsea and Jacqui checking out a rental possibility for Jacqui's art gallery. Byron called while we were there. Chelsea told me to tell you that she and Jacqui will be over shortly."

Maggie looked at Paolo, who was sitting at the kitchen table with Lexi in his lap.

"I guess she's been pretty sick for months now," Millie continued.

"Yes, I know," Maggie said.

The crackling of the seashell driveway meant Sarah had arrived.

"Hey, where is everybody?" she yelled coming through the front door.

"Back here in the kitchen," Maggie called out.

"Hey, you two," Sarah hugged Lauren and Beth. "How was your flight?"

"Uneventful, thankfully," Beth said.

Sarah looked around the room. Even Riley and Iris seemed stoic, leaning against the sink with their arms folded.

"What's going on? You all look like you just got bad news."

"We did," Maggie said. "Byron Jameson's wife, Louise, died last night."

"Oh no. Poor Byron. How is he doing?"

Maggie shrugged. "It wasn't unexpected, but I'm sure he's very sad. I think he told me once that he and Louise had never been apart, not even for one day in all the years they were married."

"I suppose it's too early to know anything about the funeral?" Sarah asked.

"Linda St. James said that she'd let us know just as soon as she heard anything. It will be in the island newspaper so she'll need to know right away."

Chelsea and Jacqui came into the kitchen through the back door.

"I can tell by the look on everyone's face that Millie told you?" Chelsea said.

Maggie nodded.

"How did Byron sound?" Paolo asked.

Chelsea shrugged. "Like you'd expect. He said that he was glad Louise wasn't in pain any longer. That gave him some comfort I think."

It was difficult to change the mood but Maggie loved that Sarah tried.

"Sorry that you arrived just when the news came in, but we're super happy to see you guys."

"How was Ciara's wedding?" Lauren asked.

Sarah put her hand to her heart. "It was absolutely gorgeous, right Mom?"

Maggie nodded. "It was indeed. Ciara looked like an angel. She and Crawford are very happy."

"How did things go with Linda?" Riley asked Jacqui.

Jacqui smiled. "Really great. I'm her new tenant."

"That's great news," Maggie said. "Do you have a name for your gallery?"

"I think I'm just going with my name. Jacqui Hutchins' Gallery. I'm thinking the sign will have my name in gold script lettering with a black background."

"I like it," Riley said.

"Me too," Sarah added. "I think it will really stand out."

"Well, is anyone hungry? We were just about to have lunch in the dining room."

"Not for me, thank you," Jacqui said. "I've got to get back to my parents' place. I want to pass on the good news."

"I'll walk you out," Chelsea said.

"Good luck, Jacqui," Millie added.

"Thanks, Millie. This wouldn't have happened if you didn't suggest it."

Maggie watched as once again Millie beamed with pride, but Maggie knew Linda St. James better than most and worried there might be trouble on the horizon.

Linda wasn't known for minding her own business, and Maggie couldn't imagine this time would be any different.

Beth unpacked her things quickly, hoping for some quiet time with her mother. The passing of her mother's friend and what seemed like a steady stream of people always coming and going from the inn made it impossible to have the privacy she needed.

At lunch everyone talked over each other and the noise finally got to her. She finished her food and excused herself. Her room was upstairs but not so far that she couldn't still hear everyone talking.

She was surprised when her mother came up behind her.

"Sorry, I didn't mean to startle you," Maggie said. "Do you have everything you need?"

"Yes, I'm fine."

"Honey, I know it's crazy around here but…"

"No, it's fine. I should have realized that your life is pretty busy. I didn't give you much time to plan. I'm sorry about that."

Maggie grabbed Beth's shoulders and faced her.

"Beth, you never have to give me time to prepare to see you. I don't care if I'm in the middle of a root canal. This is your home."

Maggie could see Beth struggling not to cry.

"Honey, what is it? Talk to me."

Beth wanted to talk but felt the time wasn't right.

"I *do* want to talk to you about what's going on in my life. It's why I came here. Maybe tonight, after everyone's gone home?"

Maggie hugged Beth and squeezed her tight.

"You are my number one priority young lady. If they don't go home, I'll kick them out," she teased.

Beth laughed. "No need to go to such lengths, Mom."

"Anyway, Chelsea and Millie just went home. Riley is leaving early for her date with Andrew tonight. The only person around will be Iris and she'll go after dinner. We should have plenty of privacy."

Maggie started for the stairs, but Beth's voice called her back.

"Mom! Do me a favor?"

"Anything."

"Make sure you've got enough tea for Lauren and Sarah too. I need my sisters too."

Maggie smiled. "I think we can make that happen."

"A sleepover?" Sarah asked her mother. "Oh, I don't know. I was supposed to see Emma before she left."

"When is she leaving?"

"Day after tomorrow I think. She and Gareth are headed to Spain and Jillian has to get back to her practice in Naples. I'll call her and see if we can do it tomorrow night or even lunch if she's busy. I'll have to call Trevor about the kids."

"Ok, do it quickly. Beth really needs all of us to be together tonight."

Maggie went outside to find Paolo. He was tending to the koi pond when she found him.

"Hey handsome, can I bother you for a minute?"

"You are never a bother," he said.

"That's the right answer," she teased. "I wanted to ask you about that bench," she said, pointing to the bench near the pond.

"What about it?"

"Well, you worked for Rose for several years before I came along. Do you have any idea how old it is?"

"No idea. It was here on my first day working here. I think Rose said that lots of the kids who lived here would sneak in and carve their initials. Rose said she used to get mad about it and had to chase the kids out. I think part of the problem was her acquiring more land."

"What do you mean…more land?"

Paolo pointed to the herb garden. "Yes, this property stopped over there. Mrs. Lane wanted to extend the property line to where it is today. I think there was some fighting among the islanders about who owned what. Eventually, she got the land she wanted, but she had to pay for it. I think the bench came with that extra land."

"Who did she buy it from? Who owned the land?"

Paolo shrugged. "That, I couldn't tell you."

Maggie was more intrigued than ever.

"You could talk to someone at the Town Hall. There are land records and it's all available to the public. Maybe Michael Saccone could help."

Maggie shook her head. "No, I don't want to bother that family right now. They're dealing with a lot and will be for a while. I'm sure I can ask someone to help me locate the information."

Paolo stopped digging around the pond and looked up at her. "Why exactly do you care who owned the land? This was a long time ago and has nothing to do with us."

"It's not really the land I'm interested in. I just want more information on this bench and if the land records can get me what I want, then I guess that's where I'll have to look."

Paolo shook his head and laughed. "My goodness, Maggie. Do you not have enough on your plate? Must you go looking for more all the time?"

Maggie laughed at his question. "Think of me as a historian. Oh, before I go. I'm having a sleepover inside the inn tonight. Sarah, Beth, Lauren and me, so no boys allowed. Lexi can come if she wants."

Paolo laughed. "That's okay. I'm pretty sure Lexi and I have other plans."

"Oh?"

"Yes, I think we'll be on the living room sofa with a few blankets in front of the tv. If we fall asleep and never make it to the bed, so be it. You girls have fun."

Maggie smiled and headed back to the inn. Fun was exactly her plan. Beth needed laughter and time alone with the women who loved her best. Her special tea would help but she knew that it was love that created miracles.

Grandma Sarah didn't bother to call Maggie, instead deciding that Lauren would answer her phone.

"Hey, Grandma. How are you?" Lauren asked.

"Never mind about me. Where are you and Beth?"

"We're at the inn. Mom told me that she called you about Beth and me coming down."

"Yeah, she did. When are you going to come visit your grandmother?"

"Grandma, we were going to come get you but Mom said you had other plans. We'll be here for five days. Of course we plan to come see you. We're just settling in here now. Is everything all right?"

"Everything is fine. I thought that I'd better call and get on your calendar. Your mother forgets to call me. I moved all the way down here thinking that I'd see my daughter more than once a month, and do you think she'd come over here? Nope. She says she's busy. Do you think it's right that she's too busy to see her own mother?"

Lauren rolled her eyes at Maggie and then put her grand-mother on speaker phone.

"I mean look at you girls. You fly to Florida just to see your mother. I live practically down the street and I never hear from her. I thought at the very least she'd call to check on me. Once a week would be fine, but instead I have to call her. I could have done that back in Massachusetts. I didn't need to move to Florida to get a phone call."

Lauren knew Beth would give her a look, but she had no other choice. "Grandma, would you like to speak with Beth? She's right here."

Beth quietly shook her head and mouthed the word "no" several times.

Putting the cellphone down on the kitchen island, Lauren walked to the other side of the room.

"Hey, Grandma. How are you?"

"I'm fine, how are you? You didn't come down to Florida to jump in the Gulf waters. You obviously needed to talk to your mother. So, what's the matter? Is that new husband of yours giving you trouble? Because if he is, I'll fly back to Boston and give him a piece of my…"

"No. Gabriel and I are fine. There's nothing wrong. Lauren

139

and I just wanted to visit with Mom and you. We miss you. When can we see you? Mom told me that you don't have your car anymore."

"That's right. I'm driving a golf cart. Everyone has them down here. I'm free tomorrow and the next day. I can't see you on Thursdays though. That's my Bridge day. Well, that and Bingo."

"Bingo? I didn't know you liked that game."

"Honey, I've been taking money from these people like it's candy. When you come, I'll show you my purse. I can barely carry the thing. Anyway, you check with your mother and call me back tonight. None of this making me wait. That's what your mother would do. Don't be like your mother."

Maggie wasn't pleased to hear her mother's complaints but there was little she could do to change her mother at this age. One thing was for sure. For better or worse all three of her daughters had a bit of her in them. There wasn't much to be done about that now.

CHAPTER 20

"*A* sleeping bag? What in the world do you need that for?" Paolo asked.

"We're all going to sleep in the main living room of the inn. Now that the last guest has checked out, we're free to hang out anywhere we want."

"So, the four of you are going to sleep on the floor even though we've got six bedrooms? It's a bed & breakfast, Maggie, remember?"

Maggie laughed. "I can't expect you to understand this. It's a girl thing. So, will you please get the sleeping bags down from the attic?"

Paolo sighed. "Can I finish my lunch?"

"Of course. I'm going to see what Iris can help me plan for food."

"Where do you want the sleeping bags?"

"Just throw them on the floor in the living room. Thanks, honey."

Thrilled that all three of her daughters were visiting, Maggie, with Iris' help, wanted to make the evening one to remember.

"Popcorn is always a good choice," Iris said.

"Good idea. I love popcorn."

"How about I make three pizzas with different toppings and you all just throw them in the oven when you're ready?"

"Oh, that's perfect."

"I made a batch of Sangria. I cut up tons of fruit to infuse the wine. It should be ready by the time you all have your sleepover. There's plenty of iced tea and lemonade and several bottles of water. What else can I get you?"

"Do we have any ice cream? We'll definitely need dessert."

"We still have strawberry and chocolate left. The vanilla is gone. There are plenty of chocolate chip cookies in the plastic bin on the counter. I think that should be enough for dessert. With all the popcorn and pizza, I can't imagine you'll have any room for dessert."

Maggie laughed. "You don't know my girls. A sleepover isn't a sleepover without cookies. Thank you so much, Iris. You've been a big help."

"No problem," Iris said, a hint of sadness in her voice.

"Is everything all right? You've been a little quiet lately."

Iris nodded. "I'm sorry, Maggie. I didn't mean to bring my troubles to work. Is it that obvious?"

Maggie put her arm around Iris's shoulder. "What's wrong?"

Iris shrugged. "Oh, it's nothing earth-shattering. My boyfriend and I broke up the other day. I guess it's still bothering me."

"Oh, honey, I'm sorry. You and Nathan have been together a long time."

"Yup, four years dating but we've known each other since middle school. It's hard but I know in time things will get better."

"Am I intruding by asking what went wrong?"

"Of course not. I guess our story isn't anything new. I'm ready to take things to the next level but he's not. I don't want him to propose if he's not ready to, but I'm getting older and I want to start a family."

"I can understand how you feel, but thirty-three is still young. You have plenty of time to have children."

"Not really. I mean, if we got married we'd want to buy a house and spend at least a year being newlyweds. I'd be thirty-five before we even started trying to conceive."

"What's holding Nathan back? He clearly must love you to be exclusive all these years."

"It's not just children. He's not sure about buying a house either. He wants to rent. I don't know how to explain this except to say that his outlook screams non-committal. It's like he wants to hold on to being a kid. I think he's afraid to grow up."

Maggie laughed. "Well I don't think that's unique for men. Maybe I'm wrong but I feel that most women are nesters. Not all, but most like building a home and family with someone they love. Men aren't always in a rush to have those things. It wouldn't surprise me if that's because they feel there is so much they want to do and getting married and having children means those adventures are over."

"I've told him that it doesn't have to be that way. I've never held him back from doing anything. If we get married, the adventures can continue, and even with a family there is so much we can do…maybe even things he's never considered." Iris shrugged. "I don't know. I hate this. I hate not being with him, but I feel like if I don't take a stand now, nothing will ever change."

Touching her cheek, Maggie smiled. "Don't rule Nathan out just yet. I have a feeling that this break might give him the time he needs to decide his future. It's good that you're prepared for it to be without him, but I would still hold out hope that he'll come around."

"Do you really think so? I do love him so much."

Maggie nodded. "I do. If he loves you as much as you do him, he'll be back."

Iris hugged Maggie. "Thank you, Maggie. You've made me feel so much better. No matter what happens, I know I'm making the right choices for myself and that's the most important lesson in all of this I think, don't you?"

Maggie nodded. "I do indeed."

———

As soon as the sun set, Maggie, Lauren, Sarah and Beth headed back to the inn.

"The Captiva sunsets never disappoint," Beth said. "You truly have found Paradise here, Mom."

"You're right, I have. I just wish I could share it with all of you."

"I love living in Florida," Sarah said, "but I miss you guys so much. I don't want to put any pressure on you, but I'm sad that our kids aren't growing up together. They know their cousins only from the occasional family visits, but it's not enough."

"It's true," Lauren added. "The memories that we've made took a lifetime to create. I identify with those memories. I'm who I am today because of my past and that past includes all of you. I'd love nothing more than to move down here, and I'm seriously thinking of telling Jeff that very thing."

"What? Lauren, are you sure? The girls have friends and a life in Massachusetts. It's not as easy as you make it sound."

"I know, Mom. Jeff and I have already been thinking of making a permanent move to another place. We've even considered moving out of the country for a while to give the girls a different experience, one that they'd never get from just reading books."

"Whoa, hang on. You and Jeff have already been planning this?" Maggie asked.

"Well, not exactly. I've been considering it, and Jeff has been resisting it."

"With good reason, I'd say."

"Come on, Mom. Don't rule it out completely," Beth added. "Lots of families are doing this."

"What do I care what lots of families are doing?" Maggie insisted. "I care about Lauren's family."

"Okay, let's calm down. I haven't said that we're moving. I've just said that we're talking about it. I'm seriously thinking about homeschooling though. Lots of bullying and other stuff that I don't like has been going on in the girls' school. I'd like to believe that the girls are safe when I send them off in the morning, but I don't and it worries me every day."

Maggie wondered if Lauren's motivation for change was the result of the strain and stress from her real estate business going up in flames a couple of months earlier.

"Lauren, the best advice I can give you is to not make any major decisions when you have so much going on. Sometimes when you're trying to navigate the course of your life, it's better to just ride the wave. Part of the fun is not knowing where you'll end up. Look at me, I'm a perfect example of that very thing. Right now, I think the best thing you can do is to focus on bringing a healthy new baby into the world. The health of this pregnancy, your body and mind is what I'm concerned about."

Rubbing Lauren's belly, Maggie continued. "I understand your desire to keep your family safe, but that starts with this little one."

Lauren nodded. "I know, Mom. I'm trying to do the best I can for everyone."

"Just don't forget Jeff in that mix," Sarah added. "He matters too."

Beth was mostly quiet as they walked back to the inn. A mob of tourists joined them leaving the beach, and with the sunset long gone behind them the stars shone bright above.

"Who's ready to get into their pajamas?" Maggie asked.

"Mom, you do remember that we're adults, right?" Beth asked.

Lauren and Sarah laughed. "She's trying to recreate our

childhood.

"No, I'm not," Maggie insisted. "Adults wear pajamas too."

Sarah patted her mother's back. "That's okay, Mom. Don't ever change. We love you just as you are."

Beth and her sisters resisted their mother's need to treat them like children but they got into their pajamas, nonetheless.

Maggie lit candles and then carried bowls of popcorn into the room and filled four glasses with Sangria. The living room floor was covered with sleeping bags and pillows, and the only thing left was to decide what movie to watch.

"Do you mind if the pizza and movie waits? I'd like to talk for a bit if you guys don't mind."

"Of course not, honey," Maggie said.

Beth looked at Sarah who smiled and gave her a thumbs up.

"You guys remember when I took a leave of absence a while back?"

"Yes, you needed some time to think about whether you wanted to work as a prosecuting attorney," Maggie answered.

"Right. Well, I've been going through some things at work that's gotten me to once again question whether this is the right career for me. It's taken me several weeks of serious introspection, but I've come to believe that this isn't what I was meant to do."

She looked at her mother for a reaction, but there wasn't any that she could see.

"I'm down here to take some time to think this through, but the truth is that I think before I left Massachusetts I already knew. I'm going to quit my job."

Her mother smiled and seemed to be waiting for more.

"Is that it?" Maggie asked.

Stunned by her mother's response, she answered, "Well, yes, I guess that's it. What do you think about what I've said?"

"What I think is that I want you to be happy. If you feel that this job isn't for you then you have my support. I'm sure we all feel the same." Maggie looked around the room for reassurance. "Right girls?"

"Absolutely. Whatever you need," Sarah said.

Lauren waited a bit before answering. "Beth, you know that we all support whatever your decision is but I think since we're all here maybe it's a good idea that you tell us what exactly is behind your decision."

Beth slowly shook her head and smiled. "Ah, there it is. My big sister wants me to dig deep and spill my guts out on the floor."

She looked at Lauren and tried not to cry. "What do you want to know? That I didn't have what it takes to put a child murderer behind bars? Do you want the details on how because of my ineptitude that same man killed another child? Is that what you want to know?"

Beth's pain was too much for Sarah. "Oh, Bethy, no."

Maggie crawled to Beth to hold her, but Beth wouldn't allow it. "Don't, Mom. Don't hold me. Please…I…can't."

Beth couldn't keep the torment she'd been living with inside one more minute. Her crying came from the deepest part of her and every part of her body shook from the release.

Maggie ignored Beth's resistance to touch and raced to hold her. Feeling like she was drowning, Beth reached for her mother's arms to stay afloat. Pure terror had a hold on her for weeks and for these few moments it had abated, leaving her with the slightest glimmer of hope.

Her family had done what she'd hoped. They'd rescued her from doubt about her value which had robbed her of all courage. What the future held didn't matter near as much as the truth that she could get through anything as long as her family was by her side.

CHAPTER 21

The next morning Maggie and her daughters were greeted by dog kisses and squeaky dog toys. Lexi zoomed from one side of the room to the other and if that wasn't enough to wake them, Chelsea, Iris and Riley made enough noise in the kitchen to wake the dead.

"Looks like a bomb went off in here," Chelsea said.

Paolo stood behind Chelsea and tried to get Lexi to stop jumping on everyone.

"Lexi! Come here!"

Beth stretched and yawned, Sarah rubbed her eyes and Lauren pushed her eye mask up onto her forehead.

Through squinted eyes, Lauren asked, "What's going on?"

Maggie laughed and looked at Lexi.

"It's okay," Maggie said. "Let her run."

"What time did you all finally fall asleep?" Chelsea asked.

"I'm not sure, maybe two o'clock? We talked for a long time and then watched a movie," Maggie answered.

"What movie?" Riley asked.

"Twister," Beth answered. "But I think I fell asleep before it was over."

Millie opened the front door and joined everyone. "Good morning. Rise and shine."

Looking at her daughters, Maggie shook her head. "She's like that every morning...without coffee."

"Did someone say coffee?" Beth asked.

"Iris and I have scrambled eggs, bacon, hash browns, fruit, muffins, coffee and orange juice already on the dining room table," Riley announced.

Lexi now was pulling a blanket off Beth and trying to carry it into the dining room.

"That blanket is gigantic next to her little body. Don't be surprised if she gets lost under there," Maggie warned.

Slowly everyone got up and walked to the table. Paolo carried Lexi to her food bowl.

"I thought I'd bring her bowl down here this morning so she could be with all of us. It seemed cruel to keep her upstairs in the carriage house when all the fun was over here," Paolo said.

Maggie smiled at Paolo and his new best friend.

"You mean that you didn't want to be separated from Lexi for even a few minutes."

Paolo looked genuinely confused.

"I don't know what you mean."

"So, what's on everyone's agenda for the day?" Chelsea asked.

"At some point we've got to go pick up Grandma and bring her here. She's already put out that we've been here two days and haven't visited her," Lauren answered.

"You know what we need?" Chelsea said. "We need to get everyone together for a bonfire on the beach tonight."

"What? A bonfire?" Maggie asked.

"Yes, we haven't had one of those in forever," Chelsea explained.

"Mom, Emma, Gareth and Jillian are leaving tomorrow. I have to see them today to say goodbye. Maybe we should have a bonfire. We can get everyone to come for an end of summer celebration."

"That sounds great except it isn't the end of summer yet," Maggie said.

Sarah shrugged. "In a way, it is. Something feels different this morning, don't you think? It feels like the end of something and the beginning of a new era. I don't know how to explain it, that's just the way I feel."

Sarah looked at Beth and smiled. "Do you feel it too?"

Beth and Lauren smiled and Maggie's heart felt full of love for her girls.

Beth reached for Sarah's hand. "I do."

"I think Sarah has a point," Maggie said. "Let's have a bonfire to celebrate. Out with the old and in with the new."

"Can Linda and I come?" Millie asked.

"Absolutely. I think everyone should be there," Maggie said. "Paolo, why don't you let Ciara and Crawford and his boys know about it. Make sure they know they're invited."

"I'll get in touch with Jacqui," Chelsea said.

"And I'll call Emma. I'll see if Debbie can stay with the kids so Trevor can join us," Sarah added.

Maggie looked at Riley. "You should invite Andrew to come. I'm sure everyone would like to meet him."

Riley blushed. "I'll ask him, but even if he can't make it, I'll be there."

"Me too," said Iris. "As a matter of fact, what are we doing for food? Shouldn't Riley and I be cooking for this?"

"Absolutely not," Maggie said. "You two are family and this is a family and friends party. I'll give a call to Jack Foley and see if we can make it a lobster bake. He owes me a favor for letting his family use the inn for free when they had their reunion. I know it's last minute, but I think I can make it happen."

"I just realized something. How are we going to pull this off and not have Isabelle Barlowe find out? If she hears we're going to have a bonfire, she'll be on your doorstep by this afternoon," Chelsea asked.

"Good point. We'll just have to take that chance. I know word spreads quickly on the island, but maybe we'll luck out and she won't hear a thing. If she shows up, then she shows up. We can't worry about her," Maggie said.

"I don't think all that smoke is good for Lexi to breathe in. I might have to keep her upstairs in the carriage house," Paolo said.

Maggie wanted to roll her eyes, but instead smiled. "You're right. I think it's safer for her to stay upstairs."

Paolo looked disappointed, and Maggie thought that it wouldn't surprise her one bit if, at the last minute, he decided to stay upstairs with Lexi to keep her company.

Looking at the clock on the mantel, Lauren said, "Mom, can you call Grandma and let her know that we're coming to get her? I think we all need to shower before we go. Tell her we'll come by around noon."

"Will do," Maggie said. "Okay everyone, let's get moving. Lots to do to get ready for the bonfire."

Riley and Iris cleared the table and Beth stopped her mother before leaving the room.

"Mom, I want to thank you for last night. I thought maybe you all might have asked me for more details about the case, but you didn't."

Maggie shook her head. "Don't you get it by now? There isn't anything that you can do to make me less proud of you than I am. Unless you feel the need to share more, all I care about is giving you my shoulder and my love."

Lauren and Sarah joined them, "Mom's right, Bethy. We're here for you through everything," Lauren said.

"That's what us Wheelers do, remember?" Sarah said.

Maggie pulled her girls into a group hug. "Okay, before we all start crying again, let's get out of these pajamas, We've got a party to plan."

Jack Foley not only agreed to help Maggie pull off a last minute lobster bake, but he offered any of his staff to help out during the event.

"Thanks, Jack. I appreciate this so much."

"No problem, Maggie. Did you get a fire permit?"

"What? No. Do I need one? I had a bonfire once before without it."

"Yeah, I know, but all that has changed. The Town Hall has implemented new rules to keep everyone safe. You should talk to someone there about it. Typically, they want a few days' notice. It's possible they'll waive that, but I don't know. They've been pretty strict about the whole thing of late. Give them a call."

Not the Town Hall again, she thought. She'd already had her fill of the place in the last couple of weeks.

"Thanks, Jack. I think I'd better go up there in person."

"Good luck," he said.

Maggie grabbed her purse and checkbook. She knew well enough that nothing got done until fees were paid.

Kelly Marshfield sat at the Treasurer's desk when Maggie reached the Town Hall.

"Hey, Maggie."

"Hi, Kelly. Listen, I've got a last minute party at the inn and we'd like to have a bonfire for the event. I understand that I need a fire permit."

"Yes, that's right, but unfortunately it's too last minute. We need a three-day heads up before we assign the permits."

"Oh, Kelly, please, this is important. Is there any way we can waive that?"

Just then, Michael Saccone walked toward them.

"Maggie, hello. We don't see you up here for months and then all of a sudden, you're here almost daily."

"Hi, Michael. I'm so sorry about your sister. Louise was such a lovely woman."

"Thank you. I believe the funeral information will be online sometime tomorrow. Can I help you with something?"

"Well, I hate to bother you but…"

"She needs a fire permit for tonight," Kelly said.

"Well, give it to her," Michael insisted.

Kelly smiled. "Yes, Sir."

"Thank you so much, Michael. Sorry for the last minute notice."

"Not at all. Glad to help. I hope you and your family have a good time."

Happy that she'd successfully resolved legal matters, Maggie left the Town Hall hoping she wouldn't have to visit the building again anytime soon.

Lauren drove onto the driveway leading to Grandma Sarah's condo and parked right behind her golf cart.

"Can you guys picture Grandma driving that thing?" Beth said.

Sarah laughed. "I actually can. I see her yelling at people to get out of her way while she's speeding down the street."

"That's generous. I see her running them over," Lauren added.

Grandma Sarah came to the door and waved them in. "Come in, come in you gorgeous creatures. Look at my beautiful grand-daughters. You all are a sight to see."

"Hey Grandma," Beth said. "You look wonderful."

"I feel wonderful. How is married life?"

"Oh, it's pretty great. Gabriel is a good man."

"I'm glad to hear it. Lauren, what about you? How are you feeling? That little baby looks like he wants to come out now."

Lauren caressed her belly. "He'd better not. He needs to wait about another ten weeks at least."

"Would you girls like some candy? I have chocolates."

"Oh, chocolate. I'll have one," Lauren said.

"Not for me. I'm watching my weight," Sarah said. "Ever since I stopped working I've been nibbling snacks all day. I've found I have zero discipline when surrounded by food in cabinets and the refrigerator."

"I'm good, thanks Grandma," Beth said.

Already scurrying around, Grandma Sarah couldn't wait to show off her decorations.

"I know you're probably in a hurry for us to leave but you have to let me show you around. Come on out back and let me show you my small garden. It's not much but it keeps me busy. It's mostly container gardening, but I like that because things won't get so overgrown that I have to work too hard to maintain it."

The yard not only had several pots of different sizes, but there were also gnomes and fairies, frogs and snails and even a sign that read "Go Away."

Beth laughed. "Grandma, whatever happened to Welcome signs?"

"You like it? I thought it said exactly what I feel. I don't want people walking on my property unless they're invited."

"I guess that makes sense," Sarah said smiling at Beth.

"This yard is the only place where I'm allowed a bit of clutter. I've got knick-knacks and such but not inside. I've become quite the minimalist. I'm not spending my last years on earth dusting. I'd rather be out having a good time."

"Well, you've certainly made the place your own. You've done a lot since we moved you in, and it looks beautiful," Lauren added.

"I guess we should get going. Any idea what your mother has

planned for tonight? Should I bring something to sleep over or is someone going to drive me home?"

"You should definitely sleep over. We'll drive you home tomorrow. Tonight, we're having a bonfire party on the beach, so pack a sweater in case you get cold."

"A bonfire? Whose idea was that?"

"Chelsea's, but we all think it's a great idea."

Grandma didn't seem convinced. "We'll see. Chelsea knows how to have a good time. Your mother, I'm not so sure."

CHAPTER 22

*T*he sun was setting on the Captiva beach horizon as people started to arrive. It was natural for strangers to walk by and show an interest in the gathering, but most said hello and kept walking.

Although he didn't know anyone, Andrew seemed cheerful and willing to mingle with the others. Riley worried that she'd have to stay near him the whole evening, but that wasn't necessary as he joined with the other men talking about golf.

Jack Foley and two of his employees joined the festivities by cooking and serving the food. There was plenty of lobster but also hamburgers and hotdogs cooked on the grill just in case someone didn't like fish.

Licking his lips, Trevor said, "I can't imagine anyone not liking lobster."

"Some people are allergic to shellfish," Sarah said.

"I'm glad I'm not one of them," Joshua added. "I could live on lobster alone."

Jacqui smiled at him. "It's nice to know you can afford it. I'll keep that in mind."

Small groups began forming and at one point in the evening it looked like the men were on one side of the fire while the women were on the other.

"Who is ready for one of my Key Lime-tinis?" Chelsea yelled out.

"I'll have one," Ciara said.

"Me too," Millie announced.

"Make that three," Linda added. "I haven't had one of these since the inn reopened, Maggie. You and Chelsea certainly know how to throw a party."

Someone suggested a game of volleyball in the dark, but even with the fire and well-lit surroundings, the guys kept losing the ball. Eventually, they gave up and started talking amongst themselves as the women moved their chairs in a circle not too close to the fire. Beth and Lauren sat on either side of their grandmother.

"Andrew is very nice, Riley," Beth said. "How long have the two of you been dating?"

"Just a couple of weeks now," she said. "I think it's going well."

"I can tell you're already in love," Grandma Sarah blurted out.

"Shh, Grandma, he'll hear you. You don't want to embarrass Riley," Lauren warned.

"Oh, I'm sorry, dear. I didn't mean to be so loud," Grandma whispered.

Grandma set her sights on Jillian. "And what about you and Finn? I don't see him here tonight. How are things with you two?"

It was clear that Grandma Sarah was going to stick her nose in everyone's business. Maggie tried to stop her but had little success.

"Mom, maybe Jillian doesn't want to talk about that in front of all of us."

"Why not?"

"It's okay, Maggie, I don't mind talking about it. Finn and I are doing okay, but we've got a long-distance relationship going and I'm not sure where we're headed. He called and said he wouldn't make the bonfire but will see me tomorrow. He's going to visit his father and brothers before we meet for breakfast."

"Why long-distance?"

"I own a veterinary practice in Naples and Finn is a pilot for an executive jet company. He travels all the time. It's complicated."

Beth remained quiet and hoped that her grandmother wouldn't single her out. With everything that she'd been dealing with, she wasn't sure she could talk about it again.

Sarah thought she'd move the conversation away from a potential awkward situation with Beth.

"Emma, I'm so glad we got to spend some time together. I'm going to miss you."

"Aww, me too. I always love coming to Captiva for a visit. Gareth and I have a lot to look forward to in Spain, but I know that I'll miss Florida."

"You're still traveling around the globe?" Grandma asked. "Now that you're married, aren't you thinking about having children? How will you be able to do that if you never stay in one place for long?"

"Grandma, leave Emma alone. She just got married. They have time to figure things out, including children," Sarah explained.

Emma didn't seem upset by the question. "It's a good question, and one that I have to spend time thinking on. Right now, I'm not sure how children will fit into our lives."

"Emma, you've always wanted kids. I remember us sitting up in our dorm room late at night talking about who we were going to marry and how many kids we were going to have. I thought you wanted at least two children. What happened to that dream?"

Emma shrugged as if the choice wasn't hers. "I don't know what will happen."

Maggie hated that her mother seemed intent on ruining the evening.

Beth tried not to make eye contact with her grandmother, but that didn't protect her from the elderly woman's assault.

"And what about you, Missy? I haven't heard much from you all evening. What's eating you, girl?"

"Grandma, leave her alone," Lauren insisted.

"It's okay, Lauren. Grandma, I'm quitting my job and have been struggling with this decision for months now. I don't want anyone to talk me out of it, so don't try."

The men had walked off somewhere and the women were silent. The only sound was the crackling of the bonfire. Jack Foley threw in more wood but mostly stayed off to the side with his two sons who helped out.

Out of nowhere Grandma Sarah said one word.

"Kintsugi," she said.

Maggie looked at her mother. "What did you say?"

"I said, Kintsugi. I've been sitting here for the last hour listening to all of you women talk about your lives and almost all of you have complained about one thing or another."

"I haven't," Chelsea said as she sipped her Key Lime-tini.

"No, you haven't but then again, you never do. Anyway, let's get back to what I was saying. I'm not here to scold any of you about your attitude, but there is one thing you all have in common. For some reason, you all seem to think that you are broken in some way."

"I do not think that I'm broken," Lauren insisted.

Grandma put her hand on Lauren's leg and tapped. "Yes, you do, my dear. I love you and your sisters to pieces, but all three of you over the last year have been unhappy with a part of your lives. I'm not saying that you're unhappy in general. It's just that here we are under the stars and you all look like the world is coming to an end. So, I reminded you about Kintsugi."

"Reminded us?" Beth asked.

"Of course. Don't you remember, when you were little we made some things in pottery class. We did that together, don't you remember? You couldn't have been more than eleven at the time."

Beth smiled. "I remember."

Grandma looked at each woman and said the word again. "Kintsugi. It's a Japanese custom of repairing things like pottery and ceramics with gold. Over time, the more breaks and subsequent repairs, the more valuable a broken item becomes. You all see brokenness as a bad thing. I see brokenness as a chance to fill in the cracks with courage, resilience, perseverance. When you come out on the other side of your pain, you'll find that you are stronger for it. That's as it should be."

A reflection of light from the bonfire on Beth's face revealed a single tear, but she wasn't the only one. Iris was crying and Lauren too.

"Mrs. Garrison, I think you'd make a wonderful addition to our pilgrimage to the cathedral of Santiago de Compostela. The people who do that walk could learn a thing or two from you," Emma said.

"Well, I'm pretty busy down here, but you tell them if they need any advice, you can give them my number," Grandma said.

Everyone burst out laughing at Grandma Sarah's response. Maggie smiled at her mother.

"Mom, I don't think you have any idea just how magical you are."

Grandma took another sip of her Key Lime-tini and nodded. "It's about time you realized that."

Riley knew the guys had walked off somewhere, but she'd hoped to find some quiet time with Andrew before the bonfire was over.

She walked up and down the beach but couldn't find him. Thinking that he'd gone home without saying goodbye, she walked to the garden and sat on the bench near the koi pond.

Tiki lights cast a warm, flickering glow across the garden.

Andrew came out from a nearby tree.

"Looking for me?" he asked.

"I wondered where you were," she answered. "It looks like you're having a good time."

He nodded. "I like your friends, but I have to tell you that between Trevor and Gareth, I feel like a slacker."

"Why?"

"Did you know that Trevor has volunteered at Oxfam International and has traveled all over the world? He was born in Alaska but moved to Florida when he was in high school. He's lived in Bolivia, Bora Bora, Australia, and Hawaii. As for Gareth, I don't think there's a place in the world he hasn't been. As an author he said he likes to visit the places he writes about. I spent most of my time listening to them."

"I take it you haven't traveled very much?" she asked.

"Not anything like what those guys have done. I mean, I've been to several European countries and a few states here, but that's it."

Riley laughed. "That's it? Ask me where I've traveled to in my life. No, better yet, I'll just share the exciting details with you. I've been to Disney World twice, gone camping north of San Francisco and, um, oh yeah, Sea World. Yup, I've been places."

She was going to tease him more but he leaned down and kissed her lips. The kiss was soft and brief. Just enough to have her wanting more. When he pulled back he looked into her eyes. "You are beautiful, Riley, inside and out."

He kissed her again only this time it was longer. She worried that the others might see them, so she pulled away.

"I'm sorry, should I have not done that?" he asked.

Blushing, she looked down and shook her head. "No, it's not

that. I'm always trying to balance being a friend and an employee. Sometimes it feels awkward."

"And kissing at your job would definitely be a mistake."

Riley worried that he thought she didn't want him to kiss her. She looked into his eyes and said, "No. Don't say that. Never a mistake, just not the right place."

Her hand rested on the back of the bench and she could feel the carvings under her fingers. She turned on the phone's flashlight to see what the image was.

"Well, look at that," Andrew said. "It appears that you and I aren't the first couple to share a romantic moment on this bench."

Grateful he didn't say the word "love" she smiled at him. "That may be true but I don't think that we should carve our names in the wood."

Andrew shrugged. "Maybe not today, but there's always tomorrow."

His words excited her but she remained as calm as she could. "I think we'd better get back with the others. I hear there's watermelon and ice cream."

Music blared from the speakers and Riley knew what that meant.

"Care to take a spin around the sand with me, Miss Cuthbert?"

"I'm going to say yes because it's dark out there and you'll never see how bad a dancer I am."

They got up from the bench and he took her hand in his. "Not to worry. I don't care what your feet do. I just want you in my arms."

CHAPTER 23

*J*illian waited for Finn to say goodbye to his family before meeting him at RC Otters for breakfast. She'd just left her sister, Emma, who was going over to Sarah's place for a few hours.

Goodbyes were never easy and although Emma had so much to look forward to in the coming weeks, Jillian hated that she couldn't predict when she'd see her sister again.

Now, it was time to say goodbye to her boyfriend, Finn, but what made matters worse was that she felt pressured to move to the east coast of Florida to be near him.

Jillian knew she wasn't ready for marriage and she had no desire to move in with him. She liked her freedom and her privacy. Explaining that to Finn was bound to drive a wedge between them.

She sat at an outdoor table and accepted a mug of hot coffee while she waited. When he arrived, Jillian waved to him.

"I'm so sorry I'm late. Leaving my family always takes more time than most. I've told you about the Powell goodbye, haven't I?"

"The Powell goodbye?"

"Yes. We start saying goodbye on the hour and then everyone keeps talking for another thirty minutes before they follow you out to your car to keep saying goodbye. It takes at least one hour from the moment you decide to leave to when you actually drive away. It's a thing."

"Oh, I see. So basically, what you're saying is that you started leaving too late to get here on time," she teased.

"Exactly," he said.

The waitress came back with a full pot of coffee and a mug. "Would you like a cup of coffee?"

"Yes, please. This will be my third cup this morning. Hopefully, I don't start shaking. So, have you ordered?"

Her stomach already in knots, she said, "No, I was waiting for you, but the truth is, I'm not that hungry. I'm fine with just coffee."

"That's okay with me. Ciara made a big breakfast this morning. Between Dad, Joshua, Luke and me, I think we've eaten about a dozen eggs between us."

Jillian hoped the warm coffee would settle her nerves, but the tension between them was palpable. They both started talking at the same time.

"I'm sorry, you go first," she said.

"No, you go."

She figured there was no other choice than to come right out and say how she felt. "Finn, I honestly don't think that I can move to the east coast. I know you've had your heart set on that, but with my vet practice, I don't want to leave. It's taken me so long to get the place up and running, I'd be throwing all that away. I'm just not ready."

His face tightened for a moment, and she could see the disappointment in his eyes. Bracing herself for his response, she reached across the table placing her hand on his.

"I care about you a lot, but I need you to understand that moving east isn't something I'm willing to do now. I love my work and the thought of leaving it behind is just too much for me."

His voice barely a whisper, he said, "I thought we talked about this. I told you that I love you and can see a future with you. Is this your way of telling me that you feel differently?"

She shook her head. "Absolutely not. I just need more time, and I need you not to pressure me on this. I don't want to make a decision that I'll regret. You wouldn't want me to move if my heart wasn't in it, would you?"

"No, of course not. I just thought we were on the same page, that's all. I don't want to lose you. If you need more time, then you've got it. But I need something from you."

"What?"

"I need to hear that you can see a future with me, and that one day, you'll be ready."

She smiled. "Of course I see a future with you. I wouldn't still be in this relationship if that wasn't the case."

"Can I ask you something else without you freaking out?"

She laughed, "I guess so but I don't like the way you're asking. Am I going to freak out?"

Shaking his head he said, "Bad choice of words. Basically, I need a little more from you."

"More?"

"Would you mind if we define the word 'future?'"

She looked down at the table and thought about his question for a minute before answering. "Look, never in a million years did I think that my sister Emma would get married. Since we were kids she'd say that marriage holds a woman down and keeps her from being the best she can be. I used to think she was overly dramatic about the whole thing. Since we were kids it didn't matter so much what she thought. But then..."

He interrupted her. "She felt the same way as an adult?"

Jillian nodded. "Yup. Look at the career that she has. I've always believed that she purposely chose work that would keep

165

her from ever settling down. But then, somehow in the middle of a retreat on this very island, Gareth comes along. No one could have predicted that."

"What are you trying to say?"

She shrugged. "I think sometimes we humans need to control everything. We plan, we strategize, we organize and then when life throws us a curveball, we lose it. We don't know what to do. I don't want that. I've never wanted that. What I know is that I love you. I only figured that out lately."

He smiled at her honesty.

"I want to keep things as they are and give us time to grow together, however that needs to happen."

He sighed and squeezed her hand. "I get that, and I'm sorry that I put everything on you to take our relationship to the next level. It's what I want, and so, I've been thinking. I'm going to see what I can do to get to the west coast more often. If things work out, I might even move back to this area. Is that too much pressure for you? Tell me the truth."

She shook her head and smiled, thrilled that he'd given more thought to their future.

"No. It's not too much. In fact, I'd like that very much."

Finn reached over the table and kissed her lightly on the lips.

When he sat back in his chair he smiled at her and rubbed his belly. "You know, suddenly I'm hungry."

Even though Emma and Gareth had checked out of their hotel, Gareth needed to stay behind and have a video conference with his editor.

"I'm sorry, Emma. It can't be helped. Please tell Sarah and Trevor goodbye. I've talked to the front desk and there's a conference room available so I'll have privacy. Take the car to

Sarah's and then text me when you're on your way back. I'll keep the luggage with me."

"I understand although I hate that you're so stressed with this book. How can there be so many changes? I'm worried that when you're done, it won't look anything like what you wanted when you started this project."

He nodded. "Tell me about it. That's what's got me so angry. I've made changes to other books in the past. I don't take issue with a few moderations, but this is getting ridiculous."

Emma put her baseball cap on her head and picked up her backpack. "I won't be long."

"Our flight leaves at three, Emma. Don't forget."

She smiled and waved as she went out the door.

Traffic on the Sanibel bridge was the usual three lanes turning into a one lane mess. She'd put the top down on their convertible rental car and enjoyed the view on both the right and left of the bridge. Motor boats and wind-surfers dotted the landscape and once she descended the bridge, picnickers filled the sandy area on both sides.

When she reached Sarah's place, Noah waved to her from up on the wrap-around deck.

Climbing the stairs, Emma said, "Hey, Noah. You look like you're having fun up there."

"Daddy is going to take me on the beach and we're going to fly my new kite. I made it."

Noah handed the kite to her. "You made this?"

He nodded. "Me and Daddy made it."

The kite, a triangular shape, was plastic and Emma thought she'd seen the design before. Where did you get the material?"

"Mommy let us cup up her tablecloth."

Emma laughed and Sarah joined them out on the deck.

"Mommy is a real trooper," Emma said looking at Sarah.

"Isn't she though?" Sarah said, handing Emma a cup. "I thought you could use a cup of coffee."

"Thanks. I didn't have one yet. I left Gareth in the room with room service. I had a glass of orange juice and scrambled eggs and never got around to the coffee."

"Why didn't Gareth come with you?"

"He had a video conference with his editor. Jillian stopped by earlier to say goodbye and then the text came in about scheduling this call. He said to tell you he's sorry he couldn't make it."

"Come inside. Trevor is going to take Noah out to fly his kite. We can watch from the other side. Debbie took Sophia for a walk and little Maggie is in her playpen."

Emma went immediately to the baby, leaned down and wiggled a toy, making Maggie giggle.

"Oh, Sarah, she is so adorable."

Trevor came into the living room and hugged Emma. "So this is it, right? You guys are leaving today?"

Emma made a sad face and sat on the sofa. "Unfortunately, yes."

"I heard you talk about Gareth. It's a shame we couldn't say goodbye."

"Yeah, he was disappointed too."

"He's a really cool guy, that husband of yours," Trevor said. "I like him."

Noah ran into the room. "Can we go now, Daddy?"

"Yup. I'm ready if you are." Trevor looked at Emma and Sarah. "Are you two going to watch us? Noah couldn't wait for Emma to get here so she can watch him fly this thing."

"Yes, absolutely," Emma said. "Let's go."

Sarah and Emma went outside and looked out onto the Gulf waters while Trevor and Noah ran down the stairs toward the beach.

"You really have the perfect life, Sarah," Emma said with a touch of sadness in her voice.

"I don't know about perfect but I'm very happy. What about you? Aren't you in that newlywed bliss state?"

Emma laughed. "Why? Am I glowing?"

Sarah shook her head. "Not really and that's why I'm asking. What's going on with you?"

Emma looked back at little Maggie and shrugged. "I know this is going to sound crazy coming from me, but I'm trying to figure out if there might be babies in my future."

Sarah's eyes went wide as she sat up straight in her chair. "Did you just say babies? I must be hearing things."

Just then, Noah yelled from the beach. "Mommy, are you watching?"

"Yes, honey. We can see you." Looking back at Emma, she said, "We'd better stand up at the railing otherwise he's going to think we're not watching him."

Emma stood and waved at Noah who waved back and ran from left to right pulling the kite along the way.

"Way to go, Noah," Sarah yelled.

"Good job, Noah, look at it go," Emma added.

"So, have you and Gareth talked about having children?"

Emma laughed. "That's the problem. We never did. I suppose it's because I live a life where there's no room for children. I've pretty much acted like I didn't want any…and I didn't, at least that's what I told myself."

She took off her baseball cap and rubbed her forehead. "I'm a mess. For years, I've been creating a life I expected to live forever. Marriage and babies just weren't something I thought about, much to my mother's chagrin. But lately…I don't know."

"Mommy!" Noah yelled. "Me and Daddy are going swimming. Can Emma come swimming with me?"

"Oh, Noah, I'm sorry, I can't. I'm going home today. I'll come back another time and we can go swimming, okay?"

Noah nodded and ran off toward his father.

"I think the first thing you need to do is talk to your husband. I don't know how Gareth feels about children, do you?"

Emma shook her head.

"Well, then. I'd say that's where you start. It's hard enough raising a family when only one person is willing to put in the work. Before you bring a child into this world, the two of you need to be on the same page."

Emma nodded. "I hear you. The only problem is that I don't want to talk about it just yet. I've got to figure out how important it is to me first, and that's something I'm not clear about."

"You're not clear about it *today*. You'll figure it out and when you are certain, then talk to Gareth."

Emma hugged her friend. "I hate saying goodbye to you."

"Me too. Promise me that you'll keep coming back? I'm not going to be able to chase after you all over the world. It looks like I'm not going anywhere so you'll definitely know where to find me."

They hugged again and Sarah walked Emma to the door. "Say goodbye to Trevor for me?"

"I will."

Emma looked at little Maggie and ran to her. She picked up the baby and held her close for a few minutes, before putting her back in her playpen. Then, walking out the door and down the stairs to her car, the lump in her throat made it impossible to say anything more.

She got into her car, put her baseball cap back on her head and waved.

———

Grandma Sarah sat at the kitchen island and watched Riley and Iris prepare lunch. Paolo had dropped off a basket of freshly harvested tomatoes, cucumbers and romaine as well as an assortment of herbs from the garden.

Maggie was busy going over bookkeeping and office paperwork with Millie, Lauren and Beth were at the beach and even Lexi was nowhere to be found.

Bored, Grandma Sarah figured that with nothing to do, she'd just sit in the kitchen and wait for someone to talk to her. When that didn't happen, she started asking Riley and Iris questions.

"So, Riley, what do you think about this boyfriend of yours?"

Riley seemed taken aback by the question. "I'm sorry, what specifically do you want to know?"

"I watched him last night. He seems like a good guy, I was just wondering if you think so too."

Iris seemed amused by the exchange but she wasn't out of the woods as far as Grandma was concerned.

"What about you?" she said, staring at Iris. "You don't have a boyfriend?"

Both Riley and Iris appeared embarrassed by the interrogation but that didn't put Grandma Sarah off their trail.

"My boyfriend and I are taking a break right now."

"A break? Is that code for the two of you actually broke up?"

Riley chuckled, and Iris glared at her.

"Okay, that's it. The two of you stop what you're doing and listen to me. I know neither of you asked my opinion on dating, and why would you? You think I'm an old woman and out of touch when it comes to men. But, you're wrong. I know a thing or two."

Millie and Maggie came into the room, and from the look on Maggie's face, she seemed annoyed with her mother.

"Mom, what are you doing?" Maggie asked. "Riley and Iris have work to do. Why don't you come outside with me and we can have some lemonade and enjoy the breeze."

Grandma Sarah nodded. "Lemonade sounds good, but first I have something to say to these girls."

Maggie rolled her eyes and looked at Iris and Riley, her face apologetic.

"Riley, I'll start with you. Andrew seems like a very nice boy. I watched how he interacted with everyone and he was polite, engaging and charming. I didn't say he was a charmer...that implies someone who isn't genuine. I believe he is."

She looked at Iris next. "I don't know what the reason is for the breakup with your boyfriend, but whatever it is, you'll figure it out. In the meantime, I want the two of you to think about what I'm going to say."

Of all the women in the room, it was Millie who seemed most interested in Grandma Sarah's advice on men.

"Whether Andrew is the one or not, or if Iris and her boyfriend get back together or she begins dating someone else, both of you need to watch for one thing in the men you allow into your life. Watch the way your men treat women. I don't mean watch how they treat you...I mean all women. If they have a good relationship with their mothers...their sisters...their co-workers...women friends...it doesn't matter. A man can bring you flowers, talk sweet to you and make you believe that you are the most wonderful person in his life. We've all been there. But, it's whether they respect and are considerate of all women that matters. Mark my words, if you overlook this, it's at your own peril."

She turned to Maggie. "Now, where's my lemonade?"

CHAPTER 24

*L*inda St. James stood in front of her building and watched as Joshua, Chelsea, Jacqui and Beth carried cans of paint and other supplies inside. She thought it might be too soon to give her opinion on what should be done to make the place presentable but it was hard to keep her opinions to herself.

"What are you looking at?" Ciara asked as she came out of Powell Water Sports.

Linda shrugged. "Looks like Jacqui isn't wasting any time getting the place up and running. It's nice that Joshua is helping her."

"Well, they have been dating for quite some time. I'm sure he just wants her art gallery to be a success," Ciara explained.

Crawford joined them on the sidewalk. "Hello, Linda. Lovely day today, isn't it?"

"Hello, Crawford," she answered, looked up at the sky and then back at her building.

"It's hot."

"You're right about that. It's going to be a scorcher, I think. I see Jacqui and Joshua are getting the place ready. It's going to be nice to look across the street and see beautiful paintings in the window. You must be thrilled about the art gallery."

"Are you implying that my newspaper business is an eye sore?"

"Not at all. It's just nice that you're adding to the place. You must admit that an art gallery is much better than leaving that space empty."

"It remains to be seen just how much better it will be. Just because Jacqui thinks she can run an art gallery doesn't mean that she can. That girl hasn't held a job in her entire life."

"Well, she *has* been away at school," Ciara added.

"Anyway, I just hope they know what they're doing over there. I don't want the place ruined. Do you hear that banging? I wouldn't be surprised to find they've put a few holes in the walls."

"I'm sure my son, Joshua, knows what he's doing, Linda. I've taught him a thing or two over the years."

Linda stopped listening to him and kept her eyes on what was going on inside the building.

"I'm a bit surprised to see Beth Wheeler there. What business is it of hers?" Linda asked.

"You mean, Beth Walker, don't you? She's married now," Ciara corrected her.

"Whatever..." Linda responded, clearly focused on the activity across the street. "I think I'm going to see what they're up to," she said as she set out to investigate.

"Oh no, here comes Linda," Jacqui said. "I can tell she's about to criticize everything that we're doing."

"Leave Linda to me," Chelsea said.

"Hello, Linda. It's nice of you to want to help. Would you like a paint brush? You could help me paint the back room. Everyone has a job to do but we can always use more help."

"I'm not here to work, Chelsea Marsden. I'm just checking to make sure everything is going smoothly. I don't want any big holes in the walls. This building is old so it might not withstand all the knocking and banging you all are doing."

"As you can see, there are no holes anywhere, and I can promise you that if one shows up, Joshua will repair it."

Joshua smiled at Linda and then went back to hammering a piece of wood.

"So, now that you can see things are working out, is there anything else we can do for you? Are you sure you don't have time to help us paint?"

Chelsea knew that Linda had no intention of lifting one finger to help but waited for her answer.

"I can see that you've already got plenty of help. I'll check in on you all later to make sure there isn't any damage."

She turned and walked out of the room and across the hall to the newspaper office.

"Thanks, Chelsea. I feel like she's going to come in here to pester me every day. I'm going to have to find a way to explain that this is now my space and I'd like her to let me run things as I see fit."

"Don't worry about Linda. If she becomes too much of a nuisance, I'll have a talk with her. Just keep your eye on making this place beautiful. She'll stop complaining when people start praising her for your success."

"What? Praising her?"

Chelsea laughed. "You might as well get used to it. Linda scurries away when people complain, but she's always front and center when there's credit to take for someone else's work. The fact is that she'll tell everyone it was her idea to rent this place to you, thereby being the main reason that your gallery is a success. And, it *will* be a success. I'm certain of it."

"I'm not sure I like the idea that Linda will take credit for anything I do," Jacqui said.

ANNIE CABOT

"Your work will speak for itself my dear, and there's nothing Linda St. James can do about that."

"I don't want all of you working in this heat. Thanks for coming out so early, but I think we should only work during the early morning hours before the sun is too strong," Jacqui said.

"You might want to crank up the air conditioning until the weather gets a little cooler," Joshua said.

Jacqui nodded and then looked at Beth. "When are you going home?"

Beth sighed. "That's a good question. I'd like to stay longer, but Lauren wants to get back home. I'll call Gabriel later and see what's going on with him. He and his brother have been working around the clock on a large furniture order. He goes to work when the sun comes up and doesn't come back home until it goes down. If I want to stay longer, he might not object."

Joshua interrupted them, "Honey, I've got to get to work. I can already see people lining up at the store. I'll catch up with you later?"

"Of course. Thanks so much for helping me, Joshua. I really appreciate it."

Looking at Beth and Chelsea, he said, "I'll see you all later. Have a good day."

After Joshua left, Chelsea patted Jacqui's back. "He's a keeper, that one."

Jacqui nodded. "I think so too, but I'm keeping Grandma Sarah's advice front and center in my brain. So far, so good."

Jacqui drove back to her parents' house and Beth and Chelsea walked toward the inn.

"So, what's on your agenda for the rest of the day?" Chelsea asked.

"Well, the first thing I need to do is call my husband."

"I heard you say that you'd like to stay on Captiva for a while longer?"

Beth nodded. "I would. I'm not sure why exactly, but I don't think I'm ready to go home. Gabriel is super busy so if ever there was a time for me to do this, it's now."

"I know your mother would love to have you stay. She hates it when her children aren't around."

Beth laughed. "Yes, well, as much as I believe that, I'm glad that she made a life for herself here. Captiva is a beautiful place and I know how much her memories here are as much a part of her as anything else. All those years that we came here on vacation, I think she was plotting how she could live here permanently."

Chelsea chuckled at that. "That's a heck of a lot of plotting, not to mention patience. But I do believe that Maggie was always destined to live on this island, just as I was. What about you?"

Beth looked confused. "I'm sorry? What do you mean?"

When they reached Chelsea's house, they sat on the steps. "What I mean is you've been here a week already and I was wondering if you've found any clarity on your future. Or are you still struggling?"

Beth looked down at the sand on the sidewalk and smiled. For the first time in weeks, she did feel content and at peace just being.

"When I came here I felt completely lost. The only solution that I could see was to get with my mother and have one of her tea-infused conversations. Although my time talking with her has helped, I think distancing myself from Boston, even for a little while, has given me the time to just breathe. I didn't even realize that I'd been holding my breath until I got here."

Chelsea nodded. "It's a slower pace here that's for sure. I think it's important not to rush. I'd give that advice to anyone...anyone who isn't needing life-saving surgery of course."

Beth smiled. "Good point."

"Your grandmother has so much wisdom in her body that I'd love to bottle it and sell it to everyone. There is truth in what she says. I think those cracks that she talked about...the broken moments? That's where you find yourself. It's where you build a life that matters. How quickly you get there isn't as important as just getting there."

"Have you found that here for yourself as well?" Beth asked.

Chelsea nodded. "My situation is a little different in that Carl and I came here because he needed a place to rest after his cancer diagnosis. We knew he didn't have long to live and his choice was to live out his last days on Captiva. We'd already bought the place years earlier and would travel back and forth over time. But in the end, this is where he wanted to be, and I wanted what he wanted."

"I'm so sorry about Carl. My mother tells me that the two of you were a real love story."

Chelsea smiled. "We were that."

They sat in silence for a few minutes before Chelsea continued.

"Beth, if I can leave you with anything, I'd want you to remember something that I've found since Carl passed. Living alone as I have for all these years, I've come to understand that we all have a blank canvas to work with any time we want to start over. I think of my life like a piece of artwork. The journey is what makes a person. We add to the canvas as we go but make no mistake we all are a work in progress. Even when we start with a new canvas, we are still on the journey. I'm loving every minute of my life. I welcome the cracks and the broken days. I'm not complete yet, and I'm still building value...still adding gold, just like your grandmother said."

Beth hugged Chelsea. "I'm so glad that you and my mother are so close. She's very lucky to have a friend like you."

Chelsea kissed Beth's forehead.

"And you, my dear, are very lucky to have such a wonderful mother and grandmother. With those two women in your corner, how can you go wrong?"

Beth smiled and looked up at Chelsea. "I've only now realized just how many women I have in my corner. I hope I can pay it forward one day."

"Oh, honey. You already do."

Beth found a quiet spot in the garden to place her call to Gabriel. Before she dialed his number, she thought about what she would say. She no longer felt conflicted about her job. She knew that Gabriel wouldn't deny her anything, much less time with her mother, but she was concerned, nonetheless.

They were a two-income family and although their expenses were minimal, she still felt guilty about not having a job. She had to be fair to her boss as well. To go back to work without the passion, dedication and commitment required to work in the District Attorney's office, she'd be lying to Mitchell, only to leave in the end.

No, she was certain the right thing to do was to give her notice today, while she still had the conviction and courage to state her position.

"Hey, babe. I was going to call you today if I didn't hear from you. How are you doing?" Gabriel asked.

"Much better. You were right to suggest that I come down here for so many reasons that I can't get into right now. I just wanted to run something by you."

"Okay, what's going on?"

"Well, how would you feel if I stayed another week? I've

already made my decision about work. I'm going to call Mitchell after I hang up with you. I'm definitely quitting. I just need more time to think about my career and what I'm going to do going forward."

"Beth, if you need another week, then take it. I miss you though. Promise you won't call me next week and ask for another?"

She laughed. "No, silly. I promise."

"Is Lauren staying too?"

"No, she's going back tomorrow. I don't blame her. Jeff and the girls need her there. I appreciate that she came down here for me, but I can't keep her away from her family forever. Plus, with the baby coming, I think she's looking tired. Although she hasn't complained, I'm sure she wants to be home."

"I'm sure you're right. Call me tonight and let me know how things went with your boss, and I wouldn't mind a couple of calls in the coming week. I don't like going so long without hearing your voice. Good luck with Mitchell. I love you."

"I love you, too, and thank you for being so understanding. I'll call you later tonight."

She ended the call and took a deep breath before dialing Mitchell's number.

Her assistant Meredith answered the call.

"Hey Meredith, it's Beth. Is Mitchell in his office?"

"Hey, Beth. When are you coming back?"

"Not for another week. How are things there?"

"Crazy as usual. You know how it is. I'll let Mitchell know you're on the phone. Hang on."

Meredith had barely hung up before Mitchell was on the line. "Tell me that you're coming into the office tomorrow."

"Unfortunately, no. I'll be in Florida for another week. I'll be back in the office next week but I thought you should know that I've made my decision. I'm quitting, Mitchell. I know it's the right thing to do. This isn't the career for me."

A brief pause on the line told her that he wasn't sure what to say to her.

"Sorry, I'm trying to think what I can say to keep you here, but the truth is that I think I already knew what your answer would be. I think I knew it before you left Boston, but I had to take a chance."

She smiled. Mitchell had been a good boss to her and she hated leaving him in a bind.

"I'll stay as long as you need me to transition whatever you've got. I just can't stay long-term. It wouldn't be fair to you or anyone who needs a real champion on their case. I can't continue the way things have been without seriously doing emotional damage to myself. I hope you understand."

"I do. I really do. This place gets to me sometimes too, and I've been on this job for more than twenty-years."

"But you're amazing at what you do, Mitchell. Honestly, I wish I had even a fraction of what you have to make this work. Thank you for everything…truly. You've been the best boss."

He laughed. "I don't know about that. I think a few people around here would argue with you. Anyway, I've got to go…got a meeting in a few. I'll see you next week."

"Sounds good."

"Take care, kiddo."

Beth hung up and smiled. Mitchell always called her kiddo, and it used to drive her crazy. Now, she was certain she'd miss hearing the name.

She leaned back and faced the sun. The air was humid and every part of her felt like she was having a hot flash. Thrilled that she had another week on the island, she anticipated more intro-spection talking with her mother, grandmother and Chelsea. For now, all she wanted was a large, cold lemonade and a dip in the ocean. After that, she'd think more about her future and how she might add more to the canvas that was her life.

CHAPTER 25

"Grandma, would you like us to go buy you a bathing suit?" Beth asked.

"What for? I'm perfectly fine wearing these pants."

"How about sandals?" Lauren asked. "Don't you have sandals?"

"I do, but I only wear them when it's cloudy."

"What? Why?" Lauren asked.

"To protect my skin from the sun. I've got Scottish skin, my love. You have no idea how sensitive it is. The slightest burn and I'll be in pain for days."

"Then why in the world would you put your sensitive, Scottish skin through the torture of a tattoo?" Maggie asked.

"It's not the same thing at all," Grandma Sarah answered.

Maggie rolled her eyes in surrender and then checked the text messages and emails on her phone.

"Who else is up for the beach?" Beth asked.

"I'll go," Lauren said. "I want to enjoy the water one more time before I leave Captiva."

"Mom? Care to join us?"

Maggie sighed, "Oh dear. Louise's funeral is tomorrow."

"I'm sorry, Mom. I know how sad you are about this. I wish I

182

had known Louise, she sounds like she was a lovely person," Beth said.

"She was. The whole thing is so unfair."

"What time is the funeral?" Lauren asked.

"Ten in the morning. What time is your flight?"

"Twelve-thirty. Beth is going to drive me and keep the rental for another week. I guess I'll be leaving before you go to the funeral."

"Do you girls think you can drive me home on your way to the airport? You go right by my place," Grandma Sarah asked.

Beth nodded. "No problem. We should leave here around nine-thirty then. Mom, I really think you should come swimming with us. It will make you feel better to get in the water. You know how much you love the beach."

Maggie nodded. "You're right. It won't help anything for me to sit around feeling glum. Why don't you all head down there and I'll join you in a few. I've got a couple of things I need to do first."

"Sounds good," Beth said.

Lauren went upstairs to get her things and Beth and Grandma Sarah waited outside on the back porch.

Maggie went into her office and then closed the door. She opened the top desk drawer and took a large, padded mailer from it. Unlocking the clasp, she reached inside and pulled out a framed photo. The image was of the photo she'd taken of the initials inside a heart which had long ago been carved into the backrest of her garden bench.

It was a risk, she knew, but Maggie was convinced that the initials belonged to Byron and Louise. How and when they were added to the multitude of others, she didn't know, but in her heart she believed she was right about the origin.

Sliding the framed picture back inside the mailer, she thought more about her plan for the photo.

I'll know what to do when the time is right.

183

She put the package back in the drawer and said a small prayer that all would be well and that she'd finally learn more about the land surrounding the Key Lime Garden Inn, and the story of her beloved garden bench.

With chairs, umbrellas and blankets laid out on the sand, the women set up their spot on the beach and settled in for the afternoon. As hot as the air was, the breeze off the water helped to cool their bodies.

Grandma Sarah closed her eyes and listened to the waves hitting the shore.

"Did you go to the beach when you were young, Grandma?" Beth asked.

"No, not much. My family was very poor, so when we weren't working to bring money into the house, we'd either go dancing or to the cinema. It was much harder for my mother having to get married and have children while a war was going on. I had a brother and a sister, as you know, and most of the hardship was before I was born. Although, we had our struggles nonetheless."

"So you were born in 1944?" Lauren asked.

"Yes, my poor mother and father really struggled, and then after the war, when so much had been bombed, it was very difficult to get out from under. They did, of course. Everyone pitched in because that's what you did back then. Neighbors helping neighbors, and since everyone was basically in the same boat, we all benefitted when someone found a way to make a success of their lives."

"But you didn't stay in Scotland," Lauren said.

Grandma Sarah shook her head. "No, it was impossible. There was no life for us there. By us, I mean your grandpa and me. So, we came to America with so much hope, just like so many others."

"How did you and Grandpa meet?" Beth asked.

"Oh, that was a story. You see, we used to have dances. Everyone in the town went to the dances if you were old enough. We were both seventeen when we first had what you would call a date at one of the dances. He asked me to dance and that was that. It wasn't that I didn't know him. I already did. We went to school together since we were children. But that dance was the beginning of many years together until he died. We got married four months later."

Shocked, Beth said, "Grandma! You were seventeen when you got married? Was that even legal?"

"Oh honey, it was indeed. Before 1929 in Scotland, you could get married at twelve years old. Can you imagine that? Then they passed a law that made it so you couldn't marry before turning sixteen."

"Holy cow! Sixteen years old. I'm just trying to picture Olivia at sixteen. There's no way I could let my daughter get married at that age. Sixteen is still a baby," Lauren said.

By now, Maggie had joined them and jumped right into the conversation.

"Can you imagine yourself getting married at that age, Lauren?"

"No way," she said.

"Times were very different back then, honey. Marriage was more of a way for a family to unload a girl, who didn't bring in much in the way of either labor or money, to another family. The truth was that I never got much affection from either my ma or pa. Both were too busy trying to stay alive and feed us at the same time."

"So you and Grandpa got on a boat and came to America, right?" Beth asked.

"Yup. I'll never forget that day. We left from Liverpool,

England. That's where we got on the ship. The Empress of England was her name. I was so nervous. I wasn't sad to leave my parents or my siblings, but I was very sad to leave Scotland."

"What was it like arriving in America?" Lauren asked.

"We didn't. We arrived in Canada. My husband had family that had already come over before us, and so that's where the ship sailed to. We stayed there for only about six months when we got an opportunity to come to America. Your grandpa grabbed that chance and so we were able to come to Massachusetts."

"You know the rest of the story," Maggie said. "My sister came first, then me, then my brother, your Uncle Michael, was the only boy."

"Much to your grandpa's dismay. He wanted all boys."

"I think I'd love to live in Scotland," Lauren said.

"You should go one of these days. You have cousins over there still. Of course I don't know them well as the older generation is all gone, but you could easily find their information. I bet they're on that Facebook thing you kids all look at."

"Oh, that sounds like fun," Lauren said. "I'll have to look up everything I can on Ancestry. That's probably the best place to start."

"Yes, and the DNA thing. You should have that test done too. I'll do it with you. I bet once we have the results lots of cousins will show up. Then once you can confirm that we're related to them, we follow up with a Facebook search. I'm going to have plenty of time coming up so let's try to find out everything we can."

"Lauren, you didn't come to Captiva just to keep Beth company, did you?" Maggie asked.

Lauren shrugged. "No, not completely. I was hoping that we could talk about things."

"Uh-oh, why does this not sound good?" Grandma Sarah asked.

"Mom! For heaven's sake, let her talk," Maggie insisted.

"I'm not really sure how to express what's been going on with me. Ever since the fire, I've felt like I'm letting Jeff and the girls down. There's been bullying and some things going on at Olivia and Lilly's school that I don't like. I've been thinking about taking the kids out of school and homeschooling instead."

"Wait a minute. Lauren, the girls absolutely love their school. Is this something new? I never heard you talk about it before."

"No, it's not something new, it's just been escalating and I don't like it. Jeff thinks that I'm overreacting and of course that infuriates me because it feels like he's sticking his head in the sand on this."

"How would homeschooling work? Are you saying that you'd give up your real estate business and be home with the girls? What about money coming in? Jeff has been a stay-at-home dad for a few years now and it seems to be working."

"Mom, the situation isn't as simple as I'm making it sound. I feel strongly that I need to do more for my children. I want them to have every available opportunity in this life and sometimes I feel that the school isn't supporting my goals for my family. I don't know how to reconcile that with them needing to stay in that school. Without homeschooling as an option, I don't know what else to try."

"Are the girls unhappy in school?" Grandma Sarah asked.

Lauren shook her head. "No, but that's not the point. As a mother, I feel that it's my responsibility to keep them safe and well-educated. What if their schooling isn't what's best for them?"

Maggie smiled. "Honey, might I remind you that Olivia and Lilly are going to the same school that you went to when you were their age? You turned out just fine."

"Times are different now, Mom."

Grandma Sarah laughed. "Said every mother throughout history. Of course times are different, they're supposed to be different. If you truly feel that the girls aren't safe, then I say, yes, it's your duty to pull them out and look for an alternative situation. My question is, are they really in an unsafe environment or is this just one bully who needs to be put in his place? I'd look into what the teachers are doing about this kid."

"That's it!" Beth exclaimed. "We send Grandma to the school to teach the teachers a lesson in manners. That ought to do it."

Maggie frowned at Beth, sending a clear message that her joke wasn't funny.

Grandma, on the other hand, thought the idea was stellar. "I'll go in there. Just try and stop me," Grandma added. "I'll have a few words with the bully too."

Maggie rolled her eyes, once again concerned that her mother was getting in way over her head.

"Let's all calm down. Cooler heads can make better decisions," Maggie added.

"It's not just about the school. I want my kids to learn about other cultures and expose them to other opportunities that they might not otherwise get from only reading books. I even thought about living abroad somewhere. Now that you've mentioned Scotland, I'm intrigued by the idea of living there."

Maggie looked about to lose her mind, and this time, it was Grandma Sarah who did her best to lessen the drama.

"One step at a time. I suggest that you learn everything you can about Scotland and its people. Then, the girls and I can video call each other and talk about what it was like growing up in Scotland after World War 2. Let them go back to school in September and Jeff and you, starting with Scotland, teach them whatever you can about other cultures and other ethnicities. Perhaps learn a new language or two, then take vacations to some of these places and speak the language. In time, you'll see that your children have been exposed to other places without losing the home that they've come to identify with. There's no crime in taking pride in where you come from, even if that place is the next town over."

"I like your grandmother's idea," Maggie said. "If you do this right, Olivia and Lilly, including that little nugget inside of you, can grow up knowing far more than their immediate surroundings. Maybe even enough to teach their own children and share what you taught them."

Grandma Sarah laughed.

"What's so funny?" Maggie asked.

"I'm laughing because Lauren could be so successful at this that her children might want to live out of the country when they're adults."

She looked Maggie in the eye. "And just like that, when you don't want them to go anywhere, they'll move to another state and leave you."

They all got the implication. Beth buried her head in her towel and tried not to laugh. Maggie, on the other hand, didn't smile at all.

CHAPTER 26

$\mathcal{M}$aggie looked in the full length mirror and turned to look at the back of her dress. She was presentable enough, but Paolo looked very uncomfortable. The heat was oppressive, making wearing a suit unbearable.

"I'm so sorry you have to wear that thing," she said to her husband. "Is it really necessary?"

"The church will be air conditioned, I'm sure," he answered. "It will be fine."

Lexi was sleeping in her dog bed and looked up at the two of them for all of five seconds before putting her head back down.

"Ciara and Crawford said they'd meet us there," Paolo added.

"Which church is this again?"

"You know the one. It's that small white church not too far from Sanibellia. I guess Louise and Byron started going there years ago. I've heard it's very nice."

"Not Catholic, though, right?"

Paolo shook his head. "No, I don't believe so. I think it's a Protestant church but I couldn't tell you the specifics."

Maggie waited while Paolo went to Lexi to deliver instructions on how she should behave.

"Lexi, we won't be gone too long. I've told you before that when we go out, I want you to be a good girl and not to get into anything. Do you understand?"

This was their new ritual any time she and Paolo were gone for any length of time, and each time, Maggie wanted to laugh.

"Do you really think that she understands what you are saying?"

"Of course she does," he answered. "Has she done anything wrong all these times when we went out?"

Maggie couldn't think of any. "No, not that I can remember."

"Well then, I would say it's working."

He smiled, seemingly pleased with his logic.

The church parking lot was packed with only a couple of spots not taken. Paolo pulled the car into the one closest to the church and turned off the engine.

"Here we go," he said.

Maggie's stomach in knots, she could barely say two words when they entered the church. Not that anyone particularly liked going to funerals, but ever since Daniel died, her heart raced any time she attended one.

Maggie pointed to the left. "There are the others," she whispered, walking toward Ciara, Crawford and Chelsea.

"Hey, when did you all get here?" she asked.

"Just before you. People haven't been congregating out here, instead rushing inside to get a seat. The pews are packed. I'm assuming it's because the air conditioning is stronger inside," Chelsea said.

"Well, I guess we'd better try to find a seat. If we can't sit near each other, we'll get together after," Maggie said.

The five of them quietly tiptoed inside as the pastor of the church was already speaking. Someone handed them a folded paper with Louise's picture on the front.

As it happened there wasn't a seat available, and none of them wanted to bring attention to themselves by walking around to find any.

"Louise's husband Byron has asked that I let you all know that tonight, at the end of Andy Rosse Lane, and in front of The Mucky Duck, there will be a sunset service to celebrate Louise's life. Louise Jameson loved Captiva's sunsets. She once told me that as a life-long resident of the island, she rarely missed a sunset. She and Byron met and spent their entire marriage on the island, and as most of you know, were pillars of the Captiva Island community. I don't think there is one person in this room who wasn't personally the recipient of Louise's good nature and grace. She was and always will be an important member of this church as her memory will live on for many years to come."

Maggie took note of the pastor's words. She already knew how beloved Louise was, but she had no idea how long she and Byron had lived on Captiva. It was something she planned to understand better in the coming days.

Several people got up to share their stories of Louise. Maggie expected at some point Byron would do the same. However, she could see where he was sitting and watched as each person got up to the pulpit. Occasionally wiping his eyes, he never moved.

A woman walked to the front of the church and sang How Great Thou Art. Two more songs followed with everyone singing along. The pastor said a few words to close the service.

When the service was over, the pastor once again reminded everyone of the sunset memorial later that day, and then as people walked out of the church, several attendants directed people to their cars in an orderly fashion.

Ciara and Crawford walked in front of Maggie, Paolo and Chelsea.

"I asked about the cemetery, but I guess she's not being buried anywhere. She's been cremated and Byron has the ashes. Do you think he'll spread some at the sunset?" Chelsea asked.

"I think that's very possible. Who's going to the sunset gathering tonight?" Maggie asked.

"Ciara and I will be there. What about you guys?" Crawford asked.

Chelsea nodded. "I'll be there."

"Us too," Paolo said.

"Okay, I guess we'll see you there, then," Ciara said as she hugged Maggie.

"I'll walk over to the inn and we can head down to the beach together, if that's all right with you guys," Chelsea said.

"Of course. Text me when you're ready to leave."

Chelsea nodded and walked to her car.

Maggie took Paolo's hand as they walked to their car.

"Did you see Byron during the service?"

"Only a little. Once everyone stood it was hard to see. Why?"

Maggie shook her head and wiped a tear from her cheek. She didn't even notice that she'd been crying. Paolo opened the car door to let her in and then got inside. Turning to her he could see her face wet with tears.

Finding a tissue in his pocket, he wiped her face.

"Hey, what's this?"

"I don't think I could live my life without you. I wouldn't want to. I can't imagine how Byron is feeling. That emptiness has to be devastating. Those two were in love. I could see it on their faces when I visited the other day."

"Byron will be okay, honey. He'll be very sad for a long time, but it will get easier with time. The pain never goes away, but he's not alone. We'll make sure he doesn't ever feel alone. I promise."

Lauren said her goodbyes to her mother, Millie, Riley and Iris, and with a quick video to her sister, Sarah. She'd packed the night before and called Jeff to make sure he would pick her up at the airport.

"Apparently, Olivia won the coveted role of Dorothy in the Wizard of Oz and she's beside herself with excitement. Jeff has prepared a combination party for my return and to celebrate her getting the best role in the play."

"That's so sweet," Beth said. "You make sure to tell her that we all are so proud of her."

As Beth pulled her car into Grandma Sarah's driveway, she and Lauren were surprised to see three elderly women standing in front of her grandmother's condo.

"Oh good, they're here," Grandma Sarah said. "Pull the car over there and let's get out."

"Grandma, what's going on? We don't have much time," Beth complained.

"I know, I know. This won't take long."

"Geri, Martha and Jan, these are two of my granddaughters. You already met my namesake granddaughter Sarah, well, these are my other two, Lauren and Beth. Their brothers Christopher and Michael are still up in Massachusetts, but I'll have them come meet you next time they're in town."

Beth and Lauren smiled and everyone shook hands.

"Oh, Sarah, they're lovely."

"Well, you can see that we're related," Grandma answered, taking credit for her granddaughters' beauty. "Their mother is very pretty too. But, make no mistake, the women in my family are very smart too. Beth is a lawyer, and Lauren owns her own real estate firm."

The women nodded their approval at Beth and Lauren's achievements.

"Grandma, I think we'd better get going," Beth said. "You don't want Lauren to miss her flight, do you?"

"Oh gracious no, of course not. But wait, I wanted my friends to show you their tattoos. Look at that!"

All three women pushed their tops to the side to expose three shoulders, all with different tattoos. Still healing from the day they were inked, each had selected small bugs for their tattoo. Geri had a butterfly, Martha a bee and Jan had a ladybug.

"Wow, those are some impressive tattoos," Beth said.

Lauren peered down at their shoulders.

"Very nice, indeed. They'll look even better once the redness and swelling goes down."

Beth wanted to kick Lauren for the sarcasm, but there was no point because the women were tickled pink at their bravery and extremely proud of their new, albeit one-step-away-from-infection, tattoos.

"Well, you girls best get on your way. Lauren honey, you kiss those girls for me, will you?"

"Of course, Grandma," she said, bending down to hug her.

"And Beth, you stop over and see me one day this week. Promise?"

"I promise, Grandma."

"It was very nice to meet you ladies," Lauren said as she walked to the car. "You all try to stay out of trouble, okay?"

The women laughed, and Grandma yelled out, "Not a chance!"

"Swipe left, swept left," Millie yelled.

"No. I think he's not bad," Linda said. "I'm going to swipe right."

"What are you two doing?" Maggie asked.

"Tinder. It's a dating app. You put in your profile and then when they match your profile with someone else's profile, then you decide if you like the way they look. If not, you swipe left, but if you like them, then you swipe right. I'm trying to explain this to Linda. She's looking for a man."

"Millie! That's not the right way to describe this. I am absolutely NOT looking for a man."

"Well what do *you* call it? You're not shopping for groceries on this thing."

Linda put the phone down and Maggie thought it quite possibly the first time she'd ever seen Linda blush at anything.

"There's nothing wrong with using a dating app," Iris said.

Everyone looked at her. "Sorry, I guess I was eavesdropping. That app has lots of seniors on it. I was surprised when I heard that. Anyway, show us the guy you like Linda. We'll tell you what we think."

Linda seemed reluctant at first, but then gave in and held up her phone.

"He has a pleasant face," Iris said.

Riley had now joined them in the kitchen.

"Linda's looking for a man," Iris repeated to Linda's exasperation.

"Can we all just agree to call this person a companion?"

Millie rolled her eyes. "Whatever. It doesn't matter what you call him. Let's keep looking. Swipe right if you want."

"What happens after you swipe right?" Maggie asked.

"Well, he has to swipe right on you, too," Millie said.

"Oh my goodness, this is too much stress. I'm going to feel awful if I swipe right and that person doesn't swipe right on me. Is this really what we've come to in the twenty-first century? Whatever happened to meeting someone in person, you both look at each other and, if you're not repulsed by them, you go on a date?"

"That rarely happens anymore," Iris said.

"That's not exactly true, Iris. Look at me and Andrew. He sat across from me in a restaurant and the next thing you know, we're dating."

"Yeah, but that's not the majority of people now. Everyone is on a dating app or they're not dating. People are too busy with their careers and stuff."

Maggie shook her head. "And I thought people were crazy for buying cars with their phones. I'm off to watch tv next door. I'm beat. If anyone is looking for me, I'll be in the carriage house. Good luck with finding a man, Linda."

Riley, Millie and Iris giggled, but Linda shook her head and kept swiping.

CHAPTER 27

*I*t had been three days since Louise's funeral, and life on Captiva Island marched along as if nothing had changed. Maggie couldn't put her finger on what kept her energy down, but she was tired and cranky.

Grateful that no one seemed to notice, she rocked back and forth on the porch swing, fanning herself. Hanging over her head was the one thing she wanted to avoid. Another visit to the Town Hall was the last thing she wanted to do but there was no way around it. The information she needed was in that building.

Perhaps in old books or online records, the land and property details would show the inn's history of ownership and the truth that Rose Johnson Lane, the previous owner, never mentioned to Maggie when Rose was alive.

Beth joined her mother on the porch. "I was just looking at the weather. It's going to cool down a bit tonight."

"Thank heaven. I think this heat has been doing a number on all of us. So, what's on your plate today?"

"I'm headed to Sarah's. We're all going to spend the day at the beach. I don't get to see Noah and the girls so I thought before I head back to Boston, I'd better get over there and visit."

"That's great, honey. The kids are going to love playing at the beach with you. They're a lot of fun."

"How about you?" Beth asked.

"I've got a couple of errands that I have to do. I'm just sitting here trying to get up the energy to do them."

"Maybe instead of errands, you should come with us to the beach. Do your errands another day."

Maggie smiled. "I'm tempted, but no, I've got to deal with this stuff today. No more putting it off. You go and have fun with Sarah. Give her a kiss for me."

Beth leaned down and kissed Maggie. "I will. You take it easy today, okay?"

Maggie nodded. "Will do." She watched Beth get into her car and drive away. Gathering her courage, she grabbed her purse and headed toward her car.

Coming out of the carriage house, Paolo stopped her. "Where are you going?"

"I've got a few errands to run. I won't be long. By the way, you never said anything about the curtains, cushions and pillows I put in the cabana. Do you like them?"

He nodded. "I love them, but I forgot to tell you that I'm not the only one who loves them. Lexi keeps taking naps in there. I don't know if it's the heat or what, but every time I can't find her, I look in the cabana and sure enough, there she is."

"I'm not surprised at all. You do realize that little girl thinks that you've built the thing just for her?"

Paolo smiled and didn't seem upset by her observation, which she'd intended as an accusation.

He shrugged, put his head down and started for the garden. "I've got lots of work in the garden today. Plus, I want to finish the landscaping around the new cottage. I'll see you later. Love you."

Just then, as if on cue, little Lexi came running from the direction of the cabana and followed behind Paolo, keeping pace with his every move.

Basket in hand, Riley came down from the porch and stood beside Maggie.

Maggie shook her head. "Look at those two. Can you even remember what life was like before Lexi came into our lives?"

Riley laughed. "Nope. Not really."

"Back again?" Kelly asked.

Maggie nodded. "Can you believe it? I'm so sorry to bother you again, Kelly."

"It's no trouble at all. Most days are pretty quiet around here. Visits are always welcome, especially from you."

"That's sweet of you to say. I hope you'll still feel that way when I tell you what I've come for. I need to do some research on the Key Lime Garden Inn's history."

"What kind of history?"

Not wanting to give too much away, Maggie said, "Well, everything and anything I should think."

"I only ask because depending on what you're looking for, I might have those records here in my office, some I'd have to look up online and others might even be in storage downstairs. If the records are before 1980, then we'll need to go downstairs if I can't get the info online."

Maggie wanted to make as little fuss about her research as possible. The last thing she wanted was for word to get around that she'd been inquiring about the inn's former owner. Since Rose's family supposedly built the property in the early years of the island's development, asking for property ownership would raise a red flag for sure.

"Can you look online and in your files to see what there is on the property? More than likely, you've got everything I need right here. If not, at least then I can decide whether it's even worth looking further."

"That's a good idea. Let's start with the surveyor books. Those are over here with the land records. It's all alphabetized. Let me see."

Kelly flipped through the books to find the Key Lime Garden Inn property lines. She turned the book around to face Maggie. "Is this at all helpful?"

Maggie looked over the lines and images and shook her head. "Well, I'm sure it all means something to someone, just not me. Is it possible that there are documents that detail what these blue-prints mean?"

Kelly smiled and nodded. "Sure enough. I've got them right in this cabinet over here. Hang on and let me find the folder for the inn."

It took several minutes before she was able to pull all of what Maggie needed. "Most of our records are only one folder per property, but it looks like there's a lot more information on your place. The folder has to stay in this office, but there is a chair and table near the window that you can use."

"Thank you, I'll do that," Maggie said. "Can I keep the book as well? It's rather large, would you mind putting it on the table and I'll carry the folder?"

"Of course," Kelly said. "Come around through that door and I'll leave it on the table. Take your time."

"Thanks, Kelly."

Hoping that Michael Saccone or anyone else she knew wouldn't see her, Maggie turned her back to the front of the building and stayed partially obscured.

For the next ten minutes, she turned pages and pages of documents that were almost identical except for the calendar changing. Most everything was as Rose had described to her, with one exception. A parcel of land on the end of her property had been purchased to add another quarter acre to the inn's property line.

The transaction took place in 1970 and the papers were signed by Robert Lane and Bertrand M. Jameson. In addition to the land, there was a small home, which was scheduled to be torn down after the purchase.

Maggie sat back in her chair and looked out the window, trying to make sense of what she'd just read.

Byron's family owned that land and a home. They sold it to the Lanes. But, why?

"Did you find what you were looking for?" Kelly asked.

Maggie smiled. "Not really. I just thought it would be nice for the guests to have as much detail on the history as possible, but it looks like I've got everything there is already."

"You and Paolo have done a lovely job with the property, Maggie, everyone says so."

"Thank you, Kelly. That's nice to hear. Well, I guess I'd better get on my way. Lots of errands to run today, although I'm thinking that I just might forget about them just this once and go for a swim."

Kelly looked around and then whispered, "It's so quiet here today, I just might do the same and leave early."

Maggie whispered back, "I think you should. My lips are sealed."

As soon as Maggie left the Town Hall, she sent a text to Byron asking him to join them for dinner later that evening. Thrilled when he'd accepted the invitation, she called Riley.

"Riley, I'm going to have Byron Jameson over for dinner tonight. Would you let Paolo know, and I'd love it if you could do that chicken piccata menu we did a few weeks ago."

"Oh, the one you said you could eat every day?"

Maggie laughed. "That's the one. I want to make the dinner special, so do it up big, would you?"

"Of course. I'll take care of it."

"What time will you be home?" Riley asked.

"I've got one more errand to run. I should be home sometime

around three. I've told Byron to be at our place at six. How does that sound?"

"No problem. Everything will be ready. I'll let Paolo know."

"Great. If you need me, just text."

Maggie ended the call, closed her eyes and inhaled the sea air. She could already feel the air cool and noticed that her energy had picked up a bit. With any luck, her next stop would do more for her spirit than anything else.

Forty-five minutes later, Maggie pulled her car in front of her mother's condo. She walked to the front door and was about to ring the bell when her mother opened the door.

"Maggie, what are you doing here?" Grandma Sarah asked.

"How did you know I was here?" Maggie asked.

"Oh, you know me. I always look out the window whenever I think I hear something. Anyway, why didn't you call? You always call before you come over, not that it's all that often."

"Mom, we have to talk," Maggie said.

Her mother looked surprised and was ready to make a snide comment, when Maggie interrupted her and said, "Sit."

Her mother did as instructed and appeared to wait patiently for Maggie to explain.

Maggie sat next to her mother on the sofa and wondered how best to start. "Mom, you and I have had this contentious relationship all my life. I've been frustrated with it and my inability to explain how you make me feel, but the time has come that I can't ignore this anymore."

"I'm not sure I know what you mean," her mother said.

"Please, let me finish before you say anything. It's taken me years to finally accept that you don't like me very much."

"Maggie, that just isn't true."

"Mom, please. Even when I was a kid, I never felt affection

from you. I internalized everything and thought that there must be something wrong with me. I kept trying to improve...to impress...to do whatever I had to do to put a smile on your face or to hear something loving come from you. But, the harder I tried, the deeper the disappointment I thought you felt with me."

"Maggie, I've never been disappointed with you. It's just, well, I wasn't raised like that...my parents never said much of a kind word or praise to me. I don't remember ever being held or hugged. Our lives were too busy trying to get along in life to worry about such things. I suppose, I might have done to you and your brother and sister what was done to me, but it wasn't because I didn't care, or love you."

Maggie had never before seen her mother cry, nor did she ever recognize hurt or pain on her mother's face. Her mother didn't talk about her own childhood, and she'd never talked about her parents with any love or nostalgia in her voice.

Until this moment, Maggie hadn't bothered to understand her mother's journey. Her mother's struggles, which were far more than financial, had influenced her behavior all her life. She'd treated Maggie and her siblings with the same disdain for emotion of any sort and left them craving affection and love into their adult years.

"I don't know if I can change, Maggie. I'm an old woman. Does it help you to know that I love you and am proud of the woman you've become? I hope it does because I came to Florida to be near the closest person in my life. I hope it's not too late for us."

Maggie had tried not to cry, but when her mother's eyes filled with tears, there was no holding back. They both let the tears fall as Maggie reached for her mother's arms...arms that didn't pull away but instead embraced her daughter with love.

Twinkling lights around the porch, gazebo, newly built cottage and Key Lime Garden Inn sign were turned on just before Byron arrived. The tiki lanterns blazed a path to the new cottage and cabana, and with no guests except family, the inn was quiet.

The air had cooled and a slight breeze kept the windchimes moving throughout the evening. Standing in front of the cottage, Maggie slid her arm around Paolo's back.

"You did an amazing job on this cottage, honey. I love the seashell path leading to it and the cabana. You're a very talented man."

"Thank you very much, Mrs. Moretti. I think it came out just as I'd hoped."

"Is Beth joining us for dinner?"

"No, she's staying overnight at Sarah's. She spent the day there playing with the kids and swimming. I bet they're having a blast with her. Beth is a lot of fun."

"How long do you think before she and Gabriel have kids?" Paolo asked.

"Oh, I have no idea. I don't think for a while. She's got a lot of growing before then. I think she's still searching for her place in the world."

"I can't believe what you found at the Town Hall," Paolo said. "I don't think Rose was trying to hide anything though. I mean, it happened so many years ago. I doubt she thought there was anything to disclose."

Maggie nodded. "I agree. What I'm surprised about though is that Byron has never said anything about it. Do you suppose he doesn't know?"

Paolo shook his head. "I doubt it. He must have been about seventeen or eighteen at the time. If they were living in that house, he would have been aware of them leaving it behind."

"I guess we'll find out tonight," Maggie said.

Riley came out onto the porch and yelled to them, "Mr. Jameson is here."

"Ask him to join us out here, will you?" Maggie yelled back. Riley nodded and went back inside.

"Well, here goes," Paolo said.

Byron walked through the garden's path and past the koi pond to find Maggie and Paolo standing in front of the new cottage.

"Wow, this place has changed. Look at this," he said.

"Hello, Byron," Paolo said, shaking his hand.

"Hi, Byron. I'm so glad you could join us for dinner."

"Me too. Thank you for inviting me. My place is pretty quiet now. Louise slept a lot toward the end, but there was always so much going on around me. The hospice nurses and people stopping by. It's wonderful to have so many people checking on us, but then, after the person dies, it's eerily quiet. I was glad to get out of the house."

Lexi rubbed up against Byron's leg, and Byron looked down to see her looking up at him.

"Well, hello there. Who is this?"

Paolo picked Lexi up in his arms and kissed her head. "This is Lexi. She now is the real owner of the Key Lime Garden Inn, but she lets us live here."

"Hello, Lexi," Byron said. "What a cutie she is."

"Would you like to see the inside of the cottage?" Paolo asked.

"I'd love to."

They all walked inside and toured the small house. Decorated in teal and peach, the rooms were a perfect representation of beach living.

"The house is one step away from living in a shack on the beach. It's just an upscale version," Paolo said.

"In other words, my husband is a beach bum and this is his way of living as close to the water as you can get without living on a boat."

They all laughed at that. Byron looked around the two rooms

and then stopped in front of a photo hanging near the door leading back to the garden.

"Where did you get this photo?" Byron asked.

Maggie came up beside him. "I took the picture. It's the initials…"

Byron interrupted her. "I know what it is."

"Those initials belong to you and Louise, don't they?" she asked.

He nodded. "We were just kids. She used to come around and we'd sit on the bench for as long as we could before she had to go home."

"Byron, that bench belonged to your family, didn't it? As a matter of fact, it sat on your family's property, isn't that right?"

He shrugged. "That was a long time ago."

"Byron, why didn't you tell us? I only just found out that you and your family lived on this property before the Lanes bought it from you."

He chuckled. "Some would say stole it from us."

"What?" Paolo asked.

"Listen, I hate to bring up old stories that have no bearing on life now. I couldn't tell you the real story even if I knew it. What I know, I only heard through gossip. My parents wouldn't tell me a thing."

"What did you hear?" Maggie asked.

"That there was a fight between my father and Robert Lane. What the fight was about I couldn't say, but what I do know is that Robert must have had something on my father. My dad was always getting into trouble. He had a gambling problem which drove my mother crazy and eventually broke up their marriage. Anyway, whatever the problem, my father sold our home to the Lanes and we had to move. We moved off-island, but I kept working odd jobs here. I had four at one time once. Whatever I could do to make enough to marry Louise and move back to Captiva just as soon as I could. My father drank himself to death and my mother died a few years later of tuberculosis. That's all I know."

"I'm so sorry, Byron. When I saw the bench, I just knew that it had something to do with you and Louise."

"Thank you, Maggie. It's funny, but now standing in this house feels strange because the view is almost exactly what I used to see when I was little. The house is practically in the same spot as our little house."

"And, the bench is still here," she said.

He nodded. "Yes, but Louise isn't," he said.

Maggie put her hand on his arm. "Yes, she is, Byron. She'll always be here and in your heart. You can come here any time you want. As a matter of fact, we thought it would be nice if you were the cottage's first guest."

"Huh? What do you mean?"

Paolo patted Byron's shoulder. "We know how quiet and lonely it must feel at your house. Why not take a few days to stay in this cottage and be with us? You can look out at the ocean and revisit memories that you maybe haven't thought about for years."

"Yes, and there's always stuff going on around here. You certainly won't be lonely. You might even tell us to leave you alone so you can have some quiet time," Maggie added.

"You would do that for me?" Byron asked.

"Of course, and when you're ready to go back home, I have a gift for you. I made another copy of the photo. You can hang it on a wall in your home."

Clearly moved by their efforts to cheer him up, Byron turned and hugged Maggie. "Thank you so much." He looked at Paolo. "Both of you. I'm really touched."

Rubbing his leg again, Lexi wouldn't leave Byron alone. He picked her up and looked into her eyes. "Louise always wanted a dog."

Maggie looked at Paolo and smiled.

"How about we go up for dinner, and we'll tell you all about how Lexi came to live with us. Maybe one of these days, we can take you over to the shelter and she can introduce you to one of her friends."

Byron let Lexi rub her nose on his neck, and then looked at Maggie. "I think I'd like that very much."

THE END

ALSO BY ANNIE CABOT

THE CAPTIVA ISLAND SERIES

Book One: KEY LIME GARDEN INN

Book Two: A CAPTIVA WEDDING

Book Three: CAPTIVA MEMORIES

Book Four: CAPTIVA CHRISTMAS

Book Five: CAPTIVA NIGHTS

Book Six: CAPTIVA HEARTS

Book Seven: CAPTIVA EVER AFTER

Book Eight: CAPTIVA HIDEAWAY

Book Nine: RETURN TO CAPTIVA

For a **FREE** copy of the Prequel to the Captiva Island Series, **Captiva Sunset** - Join my newsletter HERE.

THE PERIWINKLE SHORES SERIES

Book One: CHRISTMAS ON THE CAPE

Book Two: THE SEA GLASS GIRLS

ACKNOWLEDGMENTS

With each book I continue to be grateful to the people who support my work. I couldn't do what I do without them. Thank you all so much.

Cover Design: Marianne Nowicki
Premade Ebook Cover Shop
https://www.premadeebookcovershop.com/

Editor: Lisa Lee of Lisa Lee Proofreading and Editing
https://www.facebook.com/EditorLisaLee/

Beta Readers:
John Battaglino
Nancy Burgess
Michele Connolly
Anne Marie Page Cooke

ABOUT THE AUTHOR

Annie Cabot is the author of contemporary women's fiction and family sagas. Annie writes about friendships and family relationships, that bring inspiration and hope to others.

With a focus on women's fiction, Annie feels that she writes best when she writes from experience. "Every woman's journey is a relatable story. I want to capture those stories, let others know they are not alone, and bring a bit of joy to my readers."

Annie Cabot is the pen name for the writer Patricia Pauletti. A lover of all things happily ever after, it was only a matter of time before she began to write what was in her heart, and so, the pen name Annie Cabot was born.

When she's not writing, Annie and her husband like to travel. Winters always involve time away on Captiva Island, Florida where she continues to get inspiration for her novels.

Annie lives in Massachusetts with her husband.

Made in the USA
Columbia, SC
21 November 2024

47258177R00120